Lenny Stuck His Foot Out . . .

Mousie's back knee buckled and he flailed his arms wildly, trying to get his balance. The popcorn shot straight up in the air, his jacket went sailing over two rows of heads, and Georgina shrieked and jumped out of her seat as a paper cup of soda he'd been sneaking in landed in her lap. Mousie grabbed at a seat to keep himself from falling and knocked somebody in the back of the neck. That kid yelled, "Ow! Why'd you hit me?" and leaped out of his seat, ready to dive into Lenny's row after his attacker.

Lenny leaned forward. "Have a nice trip?" he asked pleasantly.

A *Parents' Choice* Award Book for Literature

Books by Ellen Conford

THE ALFRED G. GRAEBNER MEMORIAL HIGH
   SCHOOL HANDBOOK OF RULES AND
   REGULATIONS: A NOVEL
AND THIS IS LAURA
ANYTHING FOR A FRIEND
FELICIA THE CRITIC
HAIL, HAIL CAMP TIMBERWOOD
LENNY KANDELL, SMART ALECK
THE LUCK OF POKEY BLOOM
ME AND THE TERRIBLE TWO
TO ALL MY FANS, WITH LOVE, FROM SYLVIE

Available from ARCHWAY paperbacks

Ellen Conford
Lenny Kandell, Smart Aleck

Illustrations by
Walter Gaffney-Kessell

AN ARCHWAY PAPERBACK
Published by POCKET BOOKS • NEW YORK

An Archway Paperback published by
POCKET BOOKS, a division of Simon & Schuster, Inc.
1230 Avenue of the Americas, New York, N.Y. 10020

ISBN:0-671-50078-3

First Archway Paperback printing May, 1984

10 9 8 7 6 5 4 3 2 1

AN ARCHWAY PAPERBACK and colophon are
trademarks of Simon & Schuster, Inc.

Printed in the U.S.A.

IL 4+

For John Keller.
He definitely knows why.

Lenny Kandell,
Smart Aleck

ONE

LENNY KANDELL STOOD ON HIS toes in front of the bathroom mirror. He held the broom handle up to his mouth like a microphone.

"Lemme tell you, I was born on the sidewalks of New York. My folks couldn't afford a hospital. You think that's bad? The barber told me to use his special hair tonic and my hair would come in heavy. Only one hair grew, but it weighed twelve pounds."

There was no one else in the bathroom, but Lenny heard the laughter as clearly as he always did when he rehearsed his act.

"No applause please, just throw money. No, seriously, you're a wonderful audience and I—"

"Lenny! Lenny!"

He came down off his toes with a thud. The stage dissolved beneath his feet, his white tux turned back into a striped polo shirt, the broom handle was just a broom handle. The audience had gone home, and the only one left was his mother, yelling from her bedroom.

"Lenny, are you sweeping?"

"No, Ma, I'm wide awake." He chortled. That was a good one.

"Don't be such a smart aleck, Lenny. Give me a straight answer once."

"How about a ruler? That straight enough?"

"Okay already, Lenny. Just sweep."

Lenny made snoring sounds, but his mother didn't respond.

He opened the bathroom door. "I don't know why I have to do the sweeping anyway," he complained. "Why can't Rozzie do it?"

"Rosalind isn't home now. You are. Your sister's helping out by baby-sitting for extra money. You're helping out by cleaning. So sweep."

Lenny swept. At least, he pushed the broom around the bathroom floor. What was the point in doing much more? There was hardly any dirt, and what there was would get stuck in the cracks between the tiles anyway.

"I'm done," he said, just as the downstairs buzzer sounded. Good timing. Now his mother wouldn't have a chance to check up on his sweeping.

On the other hand, it was too late to escape. Unless he ducked out and ran down the stairs—

"There they are. Buzz back, Lenny. And put the broom and dustpan away. And open the door. I'll be right out."

Oh murder, Lenny thought. Trapped.

He stuck the broom and the dustpan in the broom closet in the kitchen and pushed the buzzer that unlocked the lobby door. Right next to the button there was a little grille, which was sort of a telephone down to the front entrance. Only it hadn't worked for years. So when your bell buzzed, you just rang back, then opened the apartment door and waited to see if it was really someone for you.

Every so often kids would fool around by pushing all the buttons at once. Then all over the apartment house, doors would open and people would come out and peer around at each other until they realized it was just a prank. After a minute or two they'd mutter about "pesky kids" and go back inside, slamming their doors.

"Ma, can I go outside?" Lenny knew what the answer would be, but he figured it was worth a try. Uncle Joe was okay, but Aunt Harriet . . . "Murder," Lenny muttered.

"You can, but you *may not*," his mother replied. She came out of the bedroom patting her hair.

"You sound just like Miss Randolph. She always says that."

"If you listened to her once in a while," his mother said, "I wouldn't have to say it so much. Didn't I tell you to open the door?"

"They're not here yet, are they?"

The doorbell rang.

"Now they're here," Lenny said, and he sprinted to get the door before his mother could answer.

Aunt Harriet stood in the doorway, looking as if she'd been waiting ten minutes for Lenny to let her in. She was frowning and her lips were set in a tight little line. Her fur scarf was draped around her neck, even though it was the end of April and quite warm.

Lenny stared at the scarf. He couldn't help it. The fur had fascinated him ever since he was little. There were two heads on the end of it, and each head had two beady little eyes gleaming from the fur. And open mouths, with pointy, dangerous-looking teeth.

When he was younger, Lenny used to play jungle soldier with Aunt Harriet's furs. They would be snarling tigers, leaping out at him as he crept through the dense undergrowth of a Philippine jungle in search of Japanese soldiers. Of course, Lenny was eleven now, and

4

getting a little old for make-believe. Besides, it was 1946 and the war was over.

Uncle Joe, smiling as usual, almost pushed Aunt Harriet through the door. "What's the matter, doesn't anyone around here say hello?"

"Where are your manners, Lenny?" his mother scolded.

"Hi," Lenny said. He didn't point out that his aunt hadn't said hello either. He knew, although his mother would never admit it, that she didn't like Aunt Harriet much more than he did. And since his mother would never admit it, he couldn't ask her why they had to visit almost every week. It was just something that started after his father was killed in the war.

"And how are you today, Lenny?" His aunt took off the fur and handed it to him to hang up. "A wooden hanger, Lenny."

She always said that. She'd been saying it for three years. Lenny knew what she was going to say next. He whispered it with her.

"Wire bends the fur."

"What did you say?" she asked sharply.

"Fine," Lenny said. "I'm fine." He draped the fur around the neck of a wooden hanger and threaded the heads and tails over the bar so it wouldn't slip off. He slid his fingers over the sleek skins and secretly felt between the teeth. Mean, he thought. Those teeth could rip a man's throat out.

5

"If you ever come out of that closet, I've got something for you," Uncle Joe said.

Lenny jumped to slam the closet door. "I'm out. What've you got?"

Uncle Joe grinned widely and held out his hands. The fingers were closed into fists. "Pick which hand you want," he said. Lenny was getting kind of old for this game, but Uncle Joe still enjoyed it, and Lenny wasn't going to argue. Especially since one of the hands always held something pretty good.

Lenny pretended to ponder awhile, as if he couldn't decide which hand to pick. Even if he picked wrong, Uncle Joe would give him the surprise anyway, but Lenny acted like it was a real life-and-death decision. His uncle got a big kick out of that.

"That one," he said finally.

"Ha ha! Wrong! Guess again."

This part was a little annoying, since Lenny figured that even if his uncle didn't realize he was too old for the guessing game, he certainly ought to realize that Lenny was old enough to know that there was only one hand left.

"Duh, let me think," Lenny said.

Uncle Joe laughed and opened the other hand.

"Wow!" Lenny yelled. "Hey, thanks, it's just what I always wanted!"

Lenny practically grabbed the gleaming black-and-nickel pocketknife from his uncle's hand. "And it's not my birthday or anything," he marveled.

"Lenny." His mother's voice was strained. "Lenny, you know I don't want you to carry a knife around. We talked about this. I'm sorry, Joe, but he can't—"

"Aw, Ma, *please*. It's a present. You can't give back a present. You don't want to hurt Uncle's Joe's feelings." Lenny backed away from his mother, the knife clenched tightly in his fingers. She wouldn't make him give it back! She *couldn't*.

He'd wanted a pocketknife for almost a year now. He'd tried to save up for one himself, but when he had half the money saved, his mother had told him he was too young to walk around with a knife.

No amount of begging or reasoning had made her change her mind. "It's not a knife, it's a *pocket*knife," he'd said.

"A knife is a knife."

"No, this is a special kind. You can't get hurt with it. It has these different blades for opening cans and cleaning out a pipe and—"

"We have a can opener and you don't smoke a pipe."

"But you can use it for all kinds of—"

"No! The subject is closed."

Now he finally had the pocketknife in his hand—and a much better one than the one he'd been saving up for. He wasn't going to give it back—not when he had it in his *hand*. That would be too mean.

He looked pleadingly at Uncle Joe. His uncle frowned. "Look, Ida, I'm sorry, I didn't realize . . . I didn't mean to cause a whole big deal. Lots of boys his age have pocketknives. Boy Scouts, for instance."

"Yeah," Lenny said desperately. "That's why they're called Boy Scout knives."

"He's not a Boy Scout," said Mrs. Kandell. "He's a boy. And he's too young to carry a knife around."

"But, Ida, what are you worried about?" asked Uncle Joe. "That's he'll cut himself? He uses a knife to cut his meat and he doesn't cut himself."

Lenny nodded frantically. "Right," he said. "I wouldn't cut myself."

"What if he gets in a fight?" his mother asked.

"What if he does? You're afraid your son is going to stab somebody?"

"Maybe they'll see he has a knife and stab him first." Mrs. Kandell looked very upset. Even thinking about Lenny fighting made her bite her lip.

"No, no they wouldn't!" Lenny cried. "I'll keep it in my pocket all the time, I promise!"

"And what if the police came by and saw the fight and found you carrying a knife? They could arrest you for having a deadly weapon."

8

"Ida, it's not a deadly weapon. It's not even that sharp. You couldn't stab anyone with it." Uncle Joe actually looked like he was trying not to laugh.

"Joe, if Ida says no, that's that," Aunt Harriet said. "She's his mother. She knows best."

Lenny shot her a look of outrage. She was always butting in, always giving his mother advice, particularly about bringing up Lenny and his sister. Even though she didn't have any children of her own, his aunt always seemed to have opinions on what was good for them. This was the first time she'd ever even suggested that his mother knew best. She sure picked a fine time to agree with her.

In fact, Mrs. Kandell looked a little startled herself. Her eyes got thoughtful. "I don't suppose if he just kept it in his room he could get into any trouble . . ." she said slowly.

"Of course not," Uncle Joe agreed.

Lenny couldn't believe it. He looked around at the three adult faces, trying to figure out why his mother seemed to be changing her mind. Because she couldn't stand to be on the same side as Aunt Harriet? Because if Aunt Harriet said no, his mother had to say yes?

He didn't try to figure it out too long. He just yelled "YIPPEE!" and hopped around the living room waving the knife in the air like a flag.

"You won't take it out of the house," his mother said loudly.

"I won't!"

"Well . . . Come and sit down and we'll have coffee and cake. Lenny, stop leaping around like a kangaroo and sit down."

"Leaping Lenny!" he cried, so charged with excitement at finally having the pocketknife of his dreams that when he did sit down, he bounced around on the chair for five minutes, unable to keep still.

While his mother sliced the cake, Aunt Harriet began to ask Lenny about school. His eyes were just about to glaze over with boredom when the doorbell rang.

"I'll get it!" He jumped up with relief.

His best friend, Artie Marks, stood in the doorway. "I have a penchant," he said, "for going out to play. Do you?"

"A penchant?" Lenny repeated.

"You know what a penchant is, don't you?"

"Sure," said Lenny. "It's what you get when you stop working."

"Not pension, *penchant*. A strong inclination."

Artie read "It Pays to Increase Your Word Power" every month in the *Reader's Digest* and was always trying to work his new words into ordinary conversation. Sometimes he had to strain a little, like when he tried to use *congeries*, *primordial*, and *execrate* all in one afternoon, but Lenny got a kick out of Artie's brain, just as Artie always howled at Lenny's jokes.

"Anyway, do you? Want to go out and play?"

"Sure. And wait'll you see what I got!" Lenny reached into his pocket and pulled out the knife. "My uncle gave it to me. Isn't it swell?"

"Wow!" said Artie. "That's some knife. Can I hold it?"

"Sure. I'll ask my mother if I can go out."

He went into the kitchen, where Aunt Harriet was telling his mother she ought to do something about her hair or she'd never find another husband. Lenny scowled. As if his mother would want anyone to replace his father! Why couldn't Aunt Harriet mind her own business?

"Ma, can I go out and play with Artie?"

"We have company, Lenny." Her voice sounded tight.

"Oh, what does he want with a bunch of old folks like us?" Uncle Joe said. "Let him be with his friends."

"All right," Mrs. Kandell said. "But you're not taking the knife, are you?"

"No, Ma, *I'm* not taking it."

He went back to the door. Artie started to hand him back the knife.

"No," Lenny whispered. "You hold it."

"Gee, thanks!"

"For a little while," Lenny added.

He was just about to go out the door when he had a flash of inspiration. Before he could think better of it, he'd opened the closet door and pulled Aunt Harriet's fur piece off the hanger. He tucked it under his arm and whispered. "Let's scram."

"You won't be too long, will you, Lenny?" his mother called.

"No, Ma. I'll be back before Uncle Joe and Aunt Harriet leave. *Definitely*."

He slammed the front door and they sprinted down the stairs without waiting for the elevator.

TWO

LENNY'S MOTHER WAS A WORRIER.

In the summer she worried about Lenny getting hit by a car while he was running across Kissena Boulevard after a Spaulding. It didn't do any good to point out that they never played stickball on Kissena Boulevard—that you *couldn't* play stickball on Kissena Boulevard, because of the traffic. She worried that someone would hit such a long ball it would travel for four blocks before it landed in the middle of Kissena Boulevard.

In the summer she also worried about Lenny drowning, getting polio, stepping on a rusty nail and getting lockjaw, getting sunstroke, and his not eating right while she was at work and Rosalind was in charge of him.

In the winter she worried about Lenny getting hit by a car that might skid on the snow and go out of control on Kissena Boulevard. She worried about colds, sore throats, scarlet fever, influenza, the grippe, and pneumonia. In between, she worried about how Lenny was doing in school.

In the spring and fall, she worried about the change of seasons, which she said germs loved and human bodies couldn't tolerate. And she worried about how Lenny was doing in school.

Even though Lenny knew that his mother didn't want him to take the knife out of the house, he also knew her worries about it were very exaggerated. None of the things she dreaded ever came true: he'd never gotten hit by a car on Kissena Boulevard, his sniffle had never turned into pneumonia, he'd never gotten lockjaw.

It was just as unlikely that the police would arrest him for carrying a knife. So while he felt a little sneaky about the whole thing, he comforted his conscience by telling himself that he hadn't lied. *He* didn't take the knife outside. Artie did.

"Give it back now," Lenny said, when they hit the sidewalk.

"Okay." Artie sighed. "I am reluctant, though. But what are we going to do with *that?*" He pointed to the fur.

"I got the greatest idea," Lenny said excitedly. "We'll go down to the vacant lot and play jungle commando, like we used to. We can take turns using the knife. This'll be the wild animals and we'll be the commandos fighting them off. Feel the teeth."

Artie stuck his finger between the teeth. "Boy, they sure are sharp."

"Yeah," Lenny said, "they could rip a man's throat out. You can carry it to the lot if you want," he added generously.

"Uh, no thanks," Artie said, backing away. "I feel a little—uh—conspicuous walking around with a fur stole."

So did Lenny, but if Artie wouldn't carry it, there was nothing to do but scrunch it up under his arm and hope none of the kids noticed it and started razzing him.

They trotted to the vacant lot and Lenny said, "You throw it at me and I'll try to stab it with the knife."

"You're not really going to stab it, are you?" Artie looked horrified.

"Aw, Uncle Joe said this knife wasn't sharp enough to stab anything," Lenny said. "But we'll just pretend. And be sure not to drop it in the dirt or my aunt'll have conniptions."

Artie threw the scarf toward Lenny and let out a bloodcurdling roar.

"Aiyee!" screamed Lenny. "A tiger! Arrghh, it's got me around the throat." He caught the fur and wrestled with it wrapping it around his neck and falling to his knees.

"It's got me! It's got me! I'm a goner!"

"Your knife, Jim! Your knife!" Artie cried. When they played jungle commando, Lenny was always Jim and Artie was Louie.

"My knife! My trusty knife!" Lenny dug into his pocket and pulled out the knife. He made stabbing motions toward his neck.

"Jim, Jim!" Artie cried. "Unsheathe the knife!"

"What?" Lenny called. "Eat the knife! Ohh! Ugh! Yikes!" Completely caught up in the deadly attack of the fur piece, he forgot about not getting it dirty, and rolled around on the brown grass and dirt, clutching at his neck.

"Unsheathe the knife! Open it. It's closed."

"Oh." Lenny felt a little foolish. He sat up and struggled to pull out the knife blade. It was pretty tight. He dug his fingernail into the little groove and tugged. Finally it popped out.

"Aha!" he yelled. "EE-GARHH!" He rolled around on the dirt again, making stabbing motions at the tail end of the stole, which dangled down toward his waist.

"OW!"

Lenny sat up. He stared at Artie, his eyes wide.

"Hey, what's the matter, Lenny?"

No, Lenny thought. I don't believe it. I *couldn't* have. I couldn't do such a dumb thing.

"Lenny, what *is* it?"

16

Lenny shook his head. "I think," he said hoarsely, "I stabbed myself."

Artie ran over to him. "Where? Let me see."

"In the stomach," Lenny gasped.

"Pull your shirt up. Let's see if you're bleeding."

Dazed, Lenny yanked his shirt out of his trousers.

Artie peered down at his stomach.

"Tell me the truth," Lenny said. "I'm afraid to look. But tell me the truth. Don't hold anything back, I can take it. Oh, my mother'll kill me. If I don't die first."

"Lenny, calm down."

"It's bad, isn't it? I know it's bad. Give it to me straight."

"Lenny, it didn't even break the skin. Hardly. There's just a little dent, that's all."

Lenny looked down at his stomach. "That's it? Just a little dent?"

"Just a little indentation. It's nothing."

"Whew! What a relief! I thought I'd nearly killed myself and you'd have to get an ambulance." For some reason he didn't understand, Lenny felt the briefest flash of disappointment.

"Well, I guess it's your turn." He unwrapped the fur piece from his neck and handed it to Artie along with the knife.

"No, you have to throw it at me," Artie

reminded him. "It's going to be a vicious cobra that leaps out from behind a rock just when I least expect—"

"Hey, a cobra with fur? That's goofy."

"I want it to be a cobra," Artie said stubbornly. "With fangs that rip and shred and tear—"

"Okay, okay already, so it's a Philippine hairy cobra. Ready?"

"Don't ask me if I'm ready," Artie said. "The cobra wouldn't ask me. He'd just pounce when I least expected it."

Lenny backed away from his friend and held the scarf by one end. He slid his fingers up a little to get a good grip on it. Suddenly, his thumb seemed to sink down into the fur and somehow, he could feel it touching his finger on the back side of the scarf.

Lenny turned pale. His mouth opened, but no words came out. He moved his thumb around, and sure enough, it went right through the front of the fur and out the other side. There was a hole in Aunt Harriet's fur stole.

For a moment Lenny actually felt his heart stop. Slowly, reluctantly, he lowered his eyes to peek at the stole, not wanting to see what he knew he'd see.

"Oh cripes," he moaned. He sank back to the ground, cradling the fur in his lap.

"What now?" Artie demanded.

"I'm a dead man!" Lenny wailed. "I'm a

dead man! I stabbed the fur. I put a hole right through it."

"What?" Artie squatted on the ground next to him. "I thought you said that knife wasn't sharp enough to stab anything."

"I didn't say that," Lenny moaned. "My uncle said that. I believed him. I figured he knew what he was talking about. He bought the knife, didn't he? Oh, what'm I gonna *do?*"

Artie peered at the hole. He stuck his finger through it. "Yup, that's a hole all right. That sure is a hole."

"I know it's a hole!" Lenny yelled. "I *told* you it was a hole! And get your finger out of it before you make it bigger."

"Maybe we could sew it up?"

"I don't know how to sew! And even if I did, you can't sew fur."

"Well, somebody must have sewed this fur," reasoned Artie, "because there are two heads on it, and I don't know of any fur-bearing animal with two heads. So they must have sewed two of these together to make one stole."

"All right, all right, so somebody, somewhere, sewed fur. Do you know how to do it?"

"No," Artie admitted.

"Well, neither do I. So *what'm I gonna do?*"

"It's dirty, too," Artie pointed out. "It's got dirt and stuff on it."

"Artie! You're as helpful as a rubber crutch!

19

Don't tell me it's dirty, don't tell me there's a hole in it, tell me what I'm gonna do!''

Artie gazed at the fur for a few minutes, as if analyzing the possibilities. He looked solemnly at Lenny. And then, finally, he said, "I don't know."

Lenny groaned in despair. He flung himself to the ground and lay on his back, the fur piece draped over his eyes. What could he do?

If he told the truth, his mother would know not only that he'd snatched the stole, but that he'd gone outside with the knife when he'd promised not to. He didn't think she'd care much for the finer point of the argument that he hadn't actually carried the knife out of the apartment himself. He suspected she'd kill him.

The only alternative to telling the truth that he could think of was to run away. But he had no money, he couldn't go back to the apartment to get his clothes—and where was he going to run with nothing but a fur scarf and a pocketknife?

He could pawn the scarf, hop a train to Wyoming, and become a cowboy—except that he had no boots, no hat, no neckerchief, no saddle, and didn't know how to ride a horse.

"It's going to get dark soon," Artie said.

"It's already dark."

"That's because you've got the fur over your eyes."

I couldn't pawn the fur anyway, Lenny thought bleakly. It's not mine. I should never have taken it out of the house, even if it wasn't really stealing.

And besides, how much could he get for a fur with a knife hole in it?

"My only chance," said Lenny, hauling himself off the ground, "is to try to sneak back into the house and hang this up again before anyone spots me. If it looks like it's never been off the hanger, Aunt Harriet might not notice the hole. At least, not for a while. Then she'll never connect it with me."

"Well, it's a thought," Artie agreed. "You better clean it off though. It sure looks like it's been off the hanger. A lot."

Lenny tried to brush the dirt and tiny twigs off the fur. It looked dusty, no matter how hard he brushed.

"Spit on it," Artie suggested.

Lenny spit on the edge of his shirt and began wiping the fur. "That looks better, don't you think? Kind of shiny?"

"Well . . . I think it looks mostly like it's got spit on it."

Lenny wiped the stole some more, until he convinced himself that it really didn't look like it had been dragged around a vacant lot. Too much.

He sighed deeply. "We better go. Might as well face the music."

There was a lump in his throat the size of the Grand Canyon. He was amazed he could talk at all. His knees wobbled as he started to walk. He was surprised he could walk at all.

He was so miserable, he didn't even mind if anyone saw him carrying the stole. He just threw it carelessly over one shoulder and trudged alongside Artie. No amount of teasing could scare him now. Not compared to what he was going to face at home, if he couldn't get to the closet before they got to *him.*

Lenny gazed down at the ground, not worrying about stepping over cracks, too depressed to look up and see what was going on around him.

Somewhere he heard the shouts of a stickball game. An occasional car chugged past. A kid shouted up to his mother for a nickel. He walked right through a chalked potsy game on the sidewalk and hardly heard the shrieks of the angry girls.

Everyone was having fun. Everyone was finishing up a nice, normal Sunday afternoon. No one had a worry in the world except him. No one in Flushing was facing certain death, except him.

This was, he knew, the worst thing that had ever happened to him.

"Hey, kid!"

"Lenny!" Artie hissed. *"Lenny."*

Lenny looked up. He didn't see anything.

"Behind you," Artie whispered. "Cheese it."

Cheese it? Lenny wondered. What was going on? You only said, "Cheese it, the cops," or something like that.

Lenny turned around. Looming behind him was a figure that seemed immensely tall, probably a lot taller than it really was.

Probably because it had on a blue uniform and a badge and a peaked cap and was carrying a nightstick.

"Say, kid, where'd you get that fur stole?"

THREE

Whenever Lenny was scared, he thought about his father.

His father had died in the war and was practically a hero. Well, maybe not actually a definite hero, but a very brave man. Lenny was sure his father had never been afraid of anything in his life. How could he have gone off to fight Hitler and Hirohito if he were a coward?

So whenever Lenny felt fear begin to prickle his skin and sneak up the back of his neck, he asked himself, Would my father be afraid of this? Since his father wasn't afraid of anything, the answer was always, No.

This had helped Lenny through a lot of scary moments.

Up till now.

Now, walking home between Artie and the policeman, Lenny didn't even ask himself the question. Why bother? His father would never have gotten himself into such a stupid mess in the first place.

Lenny had tried to explain, but he'd made such a botch of it that if *he'd* been the cop, he wouldn't have believed himself either.

"You don't think I s-stole the stole? I mean, it's not a stolen stole. I mean, m-my aunt gave it to me. I wouldn't s-steal a stole—we were just—"

Artie hadn't been much help. He'd just stared innocently at the sky and whistled "The Last Roundup."

Lenny had thought about taking the cop to the wrong building and then claiming he'd suddenly gotten amnesia and didn't know where he lived, but he'd just end up at the police station, where they'd search him, find the knife, and call his mother. And if they didn't lock him up in reform school, his mother would lock him in his room. For the next two years.

Lenny knew she'd never get over his being brought home by a policeman. All the things she'd been worrying about, all the things Lenny was sure would never happen, had suddenly happened.

Any minute now, he thought miserably, a

rusty nail will go right through my sneaker and I'll end up with lockjaw.

His mother actually shrieked when she opened the door and saw the policeman standing between Lenny and Artie.

"What is it?" she cried. "What's the matter? Are you hurt?"

"'m not hurt," Lenny mumbled.

"Come inside, before somebody sees you!"

She yanked Lenny inside. Artie and the policeman followed. She shut the door, pushing it hard to make sure it was tightly closed.

Lenny's aunt and uncle crowded into the foyer to see what was going on.

"Lenny! What are you doing with my stone marten? It's dirty!" Aunt Harriet snatched it from him.

Lenny couldn't believe it. He was standing here with a policeman, and for all she knew, he could be seriously injured, or a witness to a murder, or maybe even *accused* of murder, and all she could think about was her stupid fur.

Lenny wished he had never set eyes on that fur. Let alone Aunt Harriet.

"Then you can identify this item?" the policeman asked.

"Of course. It's my stone marten scarf. And it's *dirty!* How did it get dirty?"

At last Artie spoke up. "We were playing with it."

26

"*Playing* with it? Playing with a valuable fur scarf?" Lenny's aunt was turning bright red. He thought she might be having some kind of attack.

"We were only—"

"Then this isn't stolen property?" the cop asked.

"Who gave you permission?" Mrs. Kandell shouted. "Did your aunt give you permission?"

"The boy didn't mean any harm," Uncle Joe said. "I'm sure he didn't mean to—"

Everybody seemed to be yelling at once. Lenny wanted to clap his hands over his ears, to disappear, to crawl under the sofa, to fall through a hole in the floor and land in 2B, where Mrs. Fidler, who was deaf, might not even notice that he'd crashed onto her dinette table.

Artie's shrill voice cut through the uproar. "We were using it," he said loudly, "to add verisimilitude to the game."

Everybody stopped talking and turned toward Artie.

"Very *what?*" the cop asked.

"Similitude."

The policeman took a deep breath. "Well, as long as no harm's been done . . ."

Lenny shot Artie a grateful glance. At least now he knew he wasn't going to be hauled off to the police station, so the only things left to worry about were that a policeman had

28

brought him home, that Aunt Harriet would find the hole in the fur, that his mother would find out it was made with the knife, that she'd know he'd taken the knife out of the house—

Lenny sighed. All in all, he'd still be better of falling through a hole in the floor into Mrs. Fidler's dinette.

The policeman left, but not before Mrs. Kandell had looked up and down the hall to make sure no one would see him leave their apartment.

"We'll pay to have it cleaned, Harriet," she said. "I'm sorry about all this. And I'm sure Lenny is too. He'll find a way to apologize, won't you, Leonard?"

Lenny held his breath. Aunt Harriet was brushing off the fur, picking at it fretfully with her fingers. Any minute now she might discover the hole.

"Leonard! We're waiting for you to apologize!" His mother glowered at him. Aunt Harriet was still anxiously stroking her stole, as if it were a sick little baby who needed to be soothed. Lenny couldn't breathe. He thought he might faint, right there, right in front of everyone.

Actually, fainting might not be a bad idea, he thought.

"Not to mention that an explanation is in order," his mother added.

"We only wanted—" he began weakly.

"Never mind the excuses!"

"But you asked—"

"Ida, Ida, he didn't mean any harm," Uncle Joe cut in. "Let's forget the whole thing. Come on, Harriet, it's late. I want to get home in time for 'True Detective.' "

His aunt held the fur piece over her arm and glared at Lenny. "If you were my son . . ." she muttered.

Lenny shuddered. Perish the thought.

"Well, he's not, Harriet," Mrs. Kandell said sharply, "and I'll see that he's punished and we'll pay for cleaning the fur."

"Well, thanks for a lovely afternoon, Ida," Uncle Joe said heartily. Lenny nearly giggled in spite of himself. Some lovely afternoon!

"My pleasure," Mrs. Kandell replied. Lenny thought he might actually fall down laughing. Some pleasure!

I must be nuts, he thought. I must be cuckoo. The minute they leave, she's going to skin me alive, and I'm *laughing*. It must be shock, he decided. That's it, severe shock.

But she didn't find the hole! They were shutting the door of the apartment now, he could hear Aunt Harriet's heels clicking down the hall, they weren't turning around and rushing back, they were *leaving*. And she hadn't found the hole!

Yet.

Lenny looked down at his sneakers.

And waited.

"In all my life," his mother began, her voice dangerously soft, "I have never been so mortified."

Artie began edging toward the door.

"To have my son—my only son—dragged home by a policeman for all the world to see, like a common criminal—"

"Gee, it's getting late," Artie squeaked. "I better go home. My mother'll be worried."

Mrs. Kandell glanced at him. "It's nice to know," she said, "there are *some* boys who care about their mother's feelings." Lenny winced. Artie slipped out the door, shutting it carefully behind him.

The minute he left, Mrs. Kandell started to holler.

She hollered for a long time.

Lenny was pretty hungry by the time Rosalind came into their room carrying a plate of meat loaf, mashed potatoes, and carrots.

"I hate meat loaf," Lenny said.

"You're lucky to get anything after that dumb stunt you pulled."

Lenny knew better. His mother might yell, lock him in his room, beat him with cat-o'-nine-tails, smear him with honey and tie him to an anthill, but she'd never, never let him go without a decent supper.

"What in the world got into you anyway?"

Rozzie was talking in that stuck-up, superior voice she'd been using lately. His mother said Rozzie was fifteen, going on thirty. Lenny thought she was trying to sound like some movie star.

Whenever anyone was around, she called Lenny "my baby brother" in a sickening-sweet voice that made him want to sock her. Sure, she was four years older than Lenny, but he wasn't a baby, for Pete's sake!

And she never spoke to him sweetly when there wasn't anyone else around to hear her.

"How much does it cost to clean a fur stole?" he asked gloomily. He forgot he hated meat loaf and began shoveling food into his mouth, grateful for anything to fill up the bottomless pit in his stomach.

"How should I know?" said Rozzie. "Do I have furs?" She flopped down on her bed and reached under the mattress for the book she was reading. Lenny couldn't understand why she thought she had to hide it. He'd flipped through it once when she was out baby-sitting. It was called *Forever Amber,* and it was really boring. All historical stuff.

"Well, I gotta earn some money," Lenny said. "I have to pay to get that crummy stoned marten cleaned."

Rozzie shrieked with laughter. "Stoned marten! Oh, that's rich, Lenny!"

"Aw, dry up and blow away," he muttered.

Along with being half starved by now, and having missed all the good mystery programs on the radio, Lenny was still expecting a hysterical phone call from Aunt Harriet when she found the hole in the stole.

Hole in the stole, Lenny thought. I'm a poet and don't know it.

Poet. Wasn't there something about a poet, something he was supposed to remember? He put his plate down on the night table and frowned. Something nagged at the back of his mind. Everything before this afternoon seemed to have happened such a long time ago. But he had a good memory . . . after all, he must know a hundred jokes by heart, so it wasn't as if he were always forgetting—

By heart! That was it.

"Oh no!" Lenny groaned.

Rozzie ignored him and kept on reading.

"Oh murder!"

Rozzie frowned, but pretended to keep reading.

"Uh, Rozzie?"

"What is it already?" She stuck her finger in the book to hold her place.

"How does *Hiawatha* go?"

"What?"

"*Hiawatha*. The poem. I have to memorize twenty-two lines."

"So get your book and start memorizing."

"I can't. I left it in school."

"When do you have to know it?"

"Tomorrow," Lenny said. "But I already memorized a little of it."

"How much?"

Lenny closed his eyes and tried to concentrate. " 'By the shores of Gitche Gumee,/By the shining Big-Sea-Water.' "

"Go on."

"That's all I can remember."

"And you're supposed to know this by tomorrow?" Rozzie said.

"Yeah."

"You know what I think?"

"What?" Lenny asked eagerly. Rozzie was smart. Maybe she remembered *Hiawatha* from when she had to memorize it. Maybe she would teach him the poem and go over and over it with him until he learned it. Even if they had to stay up half the night, Rozzie might—

"I think," she said, opening her book, "you're in big trouble."

FOUR

LENNY WASN'T EXACTLY AFRAID of Miss Randolph. Then again, he wasn't exactly not afraid of her, either.

By now, Miss Randolph was used to Lenny coming in without his spelling homework, or unprepared to add $\frac{3}{8}$ and $\frac{1}{4}$ at the blackboard, or not knowing when New Amsterdam became New York.

And Lenny was certainly used to it, so he knew pretty much the worst things Miss Randolph would do to him for not memorizing *Hiawatha*. She could make him write "I must do my homework" fifty times, or give him a whole extra stanza of *Hiawatha* to memorize, or keep him after school. And since his mother

35

didn't get home from her job at Annette's Dress Shoppe until five-thirty, she never knew when he was kept after school, so he didn't have to worry about *that*.

And besides, Lenny told himself, as they walked—single file, no talking—up the steps, she probably won't even call on me. She can't have *everyone* recite the same stanza of the same poem. It would be too boring. Even for Miss Randolph. And with thirty-five kids in the class, his chance of being picked to recite was really pretty slim.

All in all, Lenny felt fairly confident as he entered the classroom. His father would never have been afraid of an old schoolteacher, and neither was he.

"Hey, Miss Randolph?" Lenny paused at her desk.

"Hay is for horses, Leonard."

"Yeah, I'm sorry. Hey, Miss Randolph, what has four wheels and flies?"

"A garbage truck, Leonard. Take your seat please."

"Darn." He couldn't stump her. He'd been trying all year. At least once a week he came in with a riddle. If Artie couldn't answer it, he figured Miss Randolph wouldn't know it either.

But she always did.

She stood there, looking somber and stern in her maroon suit and white blouse—she never cracked a smile, not even when the answer was funny. But she didn't seem to mind Lenny's riddles; she never refused to answer them and she never ignored them. Probably, Lenny thought, because she always knew the answers.

It drove him nuts.

They had reading first, which was okay, because Lenny was in the top reading group and never minded if Miss Randolph called on him. Another thing he didn't mind about reading was that he had to share a book with Georgina Schultz, who had china-doll skin and blond ringlets that bounced when she walked. Georgina was the smartest girl in the class, and everyone said she was the teacher's pet.

Lenny didn't care about that. He just liked to watch her walk.

Miss Randolph called on him to read a page aloud, and Lenny figured that was a good thing, because now maybe she wouldn't call on him again when it came time to recite *Hiawatha*.

After reading, they had a lesson on how to write business letters. Miss Randolph handed out lined paper and told them they had to write a letter of complaint.

Lenny got as far as his return address, and then spent a good part of the time trying to think up something to complain about. Finally, when Miss Randolph was just about to collect the papers, he scribbled:

Fred Allen
Hollywood,
California

Dear Mr. Allen:

I listened to your show last week and didn't think it was very funny.

Yours truly,
Leonard Kandell

The morning seemed to drag on forever.

After lunch they had spelling, arithmetic, and music appreciation. Lenny considered himself a music lover. After all, he knew most of the top songs, and was always practicing his delivery in front of the bathroom mirror. He knew a good comedian had to be able to vary his routine with a snappy tune once in a while, and the important thing about singing was not how good a singer you were, but how you could "sell" the song.

The trouble with music appreciation in school, though, was that you never got to hear very much music. Miss Randolph would play just a little bit of a record and then tell the class some sort of gimmick to remember the name of the piece and the composer.

Lenny wasn't all that crazy about the music they had to learn, because it was mostly classical stuff and nothing really catchy, but it still bothered him that they never got to hear a record all the way through to the end.

This afternoon, Miss Randolph was teaching them how to recognize *Danse Macabre* by Saint-Saëns.

"Listen carefully at the beginning and you'll hear the clock strike midnight. Listen for twelve bells."

She put on the record. Lenny listened and heard twelve bells.

Miss Randolph picked up the needle. "Remember, when you hear twelve bells, it's *Danse Macabre* by Saint-Saëns." She wrote it on the blackboard.

"We'll listen to it once more, so you'll remember it."

They listened to the first twelve bells of *Danse Macabre* again, and Miss Randolph took the record off the phonograph.

Lenny glanced at the clock. It was 2:30, and they hadn't gotten to *Hiawatha* yet.

Suddenly he wanted very much to hear how *Danse Macabre* sounded all the way through. How could they learn to appreciate music if they never got to hear any?

He raised his hand. "Miss Randolph, how come this is called music appreciation and we never really get to hear any music? We just listen to the first few notes of something. The whole year we've never heard a record all the way through. Why don't we ever to get to listen to *all* of something?"

Miss Randolph looked a little startled. She probably didn't realize, Lenny thought, that I'm such a music lover. She probably didn't think I was even listening.

"Well, Leonard, I've told you before, you all have to pass the citywide music-appreciation test this year, and what I'm trying to do is to give you some little tricks to help you on the test."

"But that's just it," Lenny persisted. "I don't see how hearing a teeny bit of a record for a test is supposed to teach us how to appreciate music."

Miss Randolph frowned. Everybody turned to stare at Lenny. They're probably surprised too, he thought, that I'm so interested in good music. Most of the other kids were really bored during music appreciation. Maybe, Lenny realized, they'd be less bored if they got to hear more music.

Lenny sneaked a look at the clock.

It was 2:35.

"We have a limited amount of time to spend

40

on music appreciation," Miss Randolph explained. "That's why we can only . . ." She let the sentence trail off. Her eyes seemed sort of faraway and thoughtful.

"Would you like," she asked suddenly, "to hear *Danse Macabre* all the way through?"

The rest of the class shifted around in their seats. Half of them looked annoyed, and the rest looked as if they couldn't care less about hearing *Danse Macabre*. Only Georgina seemed pleased.

"That would be swell!" Lenny said.

He hoped *Danse Macabre* was a long record.

Miss Randolph started up the phonograph again, and Lenny listened intently to the music. He was conscious of Miss Randolph watching him as he listened. He wrinkled up his forehead in concentration and tried very hard not to look at the clock. At least, not while Miss Randolph was watching.

Danse Macabre, Lenny learned, was not a long record. When Miss Randolph turned to take it off the phonograph, Lenny saw that the time was 2:42.

Lenny wondered if Miss Randolph would play Schubert's Unfinished Symphony if he asked her to. They'd learned it last week in music appreciation. At least, they'd learned the theme from it. Miss Randolph taught them a little song to sing along with it: "This is . . . a symphony . . . that Schubert wrote and didn't finish . . ."

Lenny knew that a symphony had to be a lot longer than a dance; why, a symphony could take up the whole fifteen minutes that was left of school. If he could get Miss Randolph to play the Unfinished Symphony, he'd bring his book home tonight and memorize the twenty-two lines from *Hiawatha* and she'd never know the difference.

He was just about to raise his hand again when Miss Randolph said, "Well, I hope you all enjoyed that," and put away the record player.

It was 2:45.

"Now we have just enough time to have our recitation of 'Hiawatha's Childhood.' "

Nothing to worry about, Lenny reassured himself. After all, I did fine in reading, and just showed all this interest in music, so she probably won't call on me again. Especially, he reasoned, with thirty-four other kids to choose from.

"I thought it might be nice," Miss Randolph said, "to have you take turns reciting the lines you memorized. Each person will say one line, and that way most of the class will get a chance to recite."

Lenny turned pale. He gulped hard, and began to scrunch down in his seat, inch by inch, trying to look inconspicuous. With twenty-two people having to recite, his chances of being called on had suddenly zoomed upward. He couldn't figure out the odds, but they were definitely not in his favor anymore.

His only hope was that Miss Randolph would call on him first. He knew the first line from *Hiawatha,* so if he got to go first—

But by the time he had thought of this and his hand had shot up, a whole bunch of kids were already straggling up to the front of the room, some of them giggling self-consciously.

Lenny quickly dropped his hand—but not quickly enough. Miss Randolph, looking enormously pleased, said, "Good, Leonard, you can be line eighteen."

Lenny wanted to kick himself. How could he have been so dumb as to raise his hand when there were only five more people to choose? She never would have noticed him if he hadn't raised his hand. Now she thought he really *wanted* to recite, and was happy because he was showing such an interest in his studies today; she was going to be twice as mad when she found out that he didn't know his line.

She might even put two and two together and decide that his sudden interest in music wasn't entirely sincere.

Lenny dragged himself up to the front of the room. He looked at the clock—2:50. In five minutes, the bell would ring. How long would it take for the first seventeen people to recite?

He took his place in the row of fidgeting kids and looked out at the thirteen lucky ones who hadn't been picked. They sat there in their seats, looking comfortable and smug; a couple had little smirks on their faces, like they were ready to burst out laughing any minute.

" 'Hiawatha's Childhood.' From *The Song of Hiawatha,* by Henry Wadsworth Longfellow," Georgina began. " 'By the shores of Gitche Gumee . . .' "

Lenny listened carefully, intently, as each person recited a line. Maybe, he thought, it'll just come to me when it's my turn. Maybe I'll remember—

How he could possibly remember something he'd never read was a disturbing thought. Maybe I can make up something. Something that sounds like it goes with the rest of the poem.

Time, 2:53.

A couple of kids forgot their lines—but only for a moment. One or two stumbled over the words, but no one went completely blank.

" 'Nursed the little Hiawatha,' " Artie recited.

" 'Rocked him in his little cradle,' " mumbled Fred Carey, sounding embarrassed.

Lenny couldn't take his eyes off the clock, so he missed the next few lines.

" 'Hush! The Naked Bear will get thee!' " giggled Ruth Bauer, who was standing right next to him.

Lenny's turn.

Naked bear? He thought. *Naked bear?*

The bell rang.

Saved by the bell! Lenny felt a whoosh of relief and started to make a run for his seat.

"Keep your places, children!" Miss Randolph said. "We have just enough time to finish. Get back in line, Leonard, and go on."

No! Lenny thought. Not fair! The bell rang.

But what could he do? He shuffled back into his place in the front of the room and looked down at his shoes. He racked his brain for anything that sounded like it would go with the line Ruth had recited.

"Leonard, we're waiting," Miss Randolph said.

Desperately, frantically, Lenny tried to think.

But he'd lost the whole sense of the poem by now, had missed the lines before Ruth's because he was watching the clock. He couldn't come up with anything that sounded like it might be part of *Hiawatha*.

"Leonard," Miss Randolph demanded, "what comes after 'The Naked Bear'?"

And Lenny said the first thing that popped into his mind, even though he knew it was wrong, it had to be wrong. But it was the only

45

thing he could think of that might come after a Naked Bear.

"A naked hunter?" he said hopefully.

When the last bell rang, everybody was laughing so hard that no one even heard it.

Except Miss Randolph.

FIVE

"NOBODY LIKES A SMART ALECK, Leonard." Miss Randolph evened up the edges of the class's business letters and stacked them in a neat pile. But she wasn't looking at them. Her eyes were firmly fixed on Lenny.

He shifted uncomfortably from foot to foot. He could hear the shouts of the kids playing in the schoolyard. Artie was down there somewhere. He'd promised to wait for Lenny, even if the wait was "interminable."

"I wasn't trying to be a smart aleck, Miss Randolph. Honest. I just said the first thing I could think of."

"Then you should learn to think before you speak."

"I did," Lenny mumbled. "I thought a long time."

"If you'd memorized what you were supposed to," Miss Randolph said sharply, "you wouldn't have had to think so hard to come up with such a silly answer."

There was no reply to that. Miss Randolph was right.

"It's not as if I forced you to recite. You raised your hand. I'm disappointed in you, Leonard. For more reasons than one."

Lenny knew what she meant.

Suddenly he felt very strange. He was used to Miss Randolph's being angry or sarcastic; he was used to being scolded, or punished, or lectured. He wasn't used to the look of weary resignation in Miss Randolph's eyes.

"You're a smart boy," she said. "If you used your head more and your mouth less, you could make something of yourself."

"Yes, Miss Randolph." Lenny knew what he wanted to make of himself. And he was sure that learning *Hiawatha* and adding fractions and knowing state capitals had not made Jack Benny or Eddie Cantor big stars.

"That's all, Leonard. You may go."

Startled, Lenny just stood there for a moment, not sure he'd heard right. That's all? He could go? Wasn't she going to make him write something fifty times, or do extra memorizing, or *something?*

"I can go?" he asked uncertainly.

"You may."

48

"Gee, thanks!"

Lenny made a dash for the door before she could change her mind. He couldn't believe he'd gotten off so easy. He felt light-headed as he sprinted down the hall to the stairs. He took the first flights two at a time. Then, suddenly, on the landing between the third and the second floor, that strange feeling washed over him again.

Sure he was relieved that Miss Randolph hadn't done anything to him, but in a little corner of his mind he was uneasy. Lenny realized that somehow, for some odd reason, part of him would have felt *more* relieved if she'd had him write "I must do my homework" fifty times on the blackboard.

"Cuckoo," Lenny told himself. But he couldn't shake off the discomfort.

He walked down the last flights of steps slowly.

It's like with Aunt Harriet's stole, he thought. It's like when you expect something awful to happen and it doesn't happen, but you keep waiting for it anyway. Like he'd waited for the phone to ring last night.

"Cuckoo," he repeated, and firmly pushed Miss Randolph out of his thoughts.

Artie was sitting on the front steps, drawing a picture of a diving Messerschmidt in his notebook.

"What happened?"

"Nothing," Lenny said. "She just yelled at me a little." Miss Randolph hadn't yelled at all, but somehow it made Lenny feel better to say that.

Artie closed his notebook. "How providential for you," he said, "that she showed clemency—even if she was vociferous about it." He looked enormously pleased with himself.

Lenny recognized that look. Three in one sentence! And Artie didn't even seem to be forcing them. "Say, not bad," Lenny remarked.

They trotted down the steps. "Hey, did you hear the one about the two sheep?" asked Lenny.

Artie shook his head. He was already smiling in anticipation.

"Well, there are these two sheep grazing in a pasture. The first sheep says, 'Baa.' And the second sheep says, 'Moo.' So the first sheep says, 'What do you mean, moo? Sheep don't say moo, they say baa.' And the second sheep says, 'I know, I know. I was just practicing a foreign language.' "

Artie didn't stop cackling for two blocks. Artie was really a wonderful audience.

"Rozzie, can I borrow a dime for the movies?"

She was doing her hair, putting some kind of goopy stuff on it and winding it around little

50

metal curlers. "What am I, Rockefeller?" She stuck two curlers in her mouth to hold them, so she could use both hands.

In fact, Lenny thought Rozzie was the closest thing to Rockefeller he knew. With all the baby-sitting she did, Rozzie was rolling in money. And she was such a miser, she hardly ever spent any of it—at least, not that Lenny noticed. She must have piles of quarters socked away in her underwear drawer, and all he needed was one crummy dime.

But Lenny didn't think it would be helpful to point any of this out.

"I'll pay you back," he promised.

"Ha ha. That's a laugh. With what? You already owe for Aunt Harriet's fur cleaning and you haven't a penny to your name."

That wasn't exactly true. Lenny had a nickel; with a dime from Rozzie he'd have just enough for the movies. He wouldn't be able to buy any popcorn, but Artie would share.

"If someone would tell me what it costs to have the fur cleaned, I'd start earning the money to pay for it."

Rozzie snickered.

"But no one tells me. Every time I ask Ma, she just says, 'We'll see.' " For a few days it drove Lenny nuts. He had no idea what cleaning a fur stole could possibly cost—let alone fixing a hole, if they found it. So the wildest figures jumped around in his head. Could it be as little as a dollar? As much as five dollars? *Even more than five dollars?*

Lenny would shudder every time he thought about how much five dollars was. Half a year's allowance.

But by Thursday, no hysterical phone call had come from Aunt Harriet, his mother hadn't mentioned policemen or furs for a whole day, and no one had come to present him with a bill for the cleaning (and possibly patching) of one fur stole.

It was just possible that everyone wanted to forget it, that the hole would never be discovered, and that Uncle Joe had convinced Aunt Harriet and Lenny's mother that Lenny had suffered enough. Lenny certainly thought he had suffered enough; there was no point, he reasoned, in dwelling on awful possibilities that might never come to pass.

Lenny had determined to put the whole thing out of his mind.

"It seems to me," Rozzie said, "that you should be out earning money, not spending it."

"I will," Lenny said, "I really will. After today. And I'll pay you back first, before anything, if you'll just *lend me the dime.*"

"Oh, all right." Rozzie slapped a curler down on the dressing table. "Anything to get you out of my hair."

"Out of your hair! Heh heh, that's a good

one," Lenny chuckled. "Get it?" He pointed to the curlers.

He was filled with gratitude toward his sister, even if she *had* made him suffer a little before handing over the dime. After all, she could have made him suffer a lot and not given him the dime at all. Rozzie was moody and unpredictable, and Lenny never knew whether buttering her up would work or just irritate her.

"Did you hear about the baby that was fed on elephant's milk and gained twenty pounds in a week?" Lenny asked. It wouldn't hurt to keep her in a good mood until he had the dime safely in his pocket.

"That's ridiculous." She pulled the red change purse from her underwear drawer and carefully picked out a dime. She stuck the purse back under a jumble of slips.

"No, really. They fed this baby on elephant milk and it gained twenty pounds in a week."

"What baby?" Rozzie demanded.

"The elephant's baby."

Lenny grabbed the dime and ran.

Ordinarily Mrs. Kandell gave Lenny money for the movies, because he only got twenty cents' allowance. Lenny's mother had to work Saturdays at Annette's, and it made her feel better to know that for at least a couple of hours on Saturday she didn't have to worry about where he was or what was happening to him. What could be safer than sitting in the Keith, quietly watching a movie? They even had a matron who wore a white uniform and kept a stern eye on the children's section.

This week, however, Mrs. Kandell hadn't given Lenny his movie money. Considering that for most of the week she'd given him nothing besides supper, orders, and an occasional pained look, Lenny didn't think it would be wise to mention the money.

Artie was waiting for him downstairs in the lobby.

"I got it!" Lenny held up the dime. "Let's go."

"Your sister was feeling magnanimous today," Artie commented.

"Yeah, but she gave me the dime anyway."

They crossed the street and headed for Kissena Boulevard. Lenny started to tell Artie the one about the tap-dancing fly. Artie began to giggle even before Lenny had finished the first line of the joke.

Artie was really a terrific audience.

Lenny looked forward to going to the movies every week. He enjoyed a good western, or a war movie—a picture with lots of action and a minimum of lovey-dovey stuff. Watching a movie like that, Lenny could really get caught up in the story and imagine himself as the hero, single-handedly wiping out a German machine-gun nest or riding a galloping white horse across the western plains in pursuit of the Dalton gang.

But while he often pictured himself in the hero's boots, Lenny never really dreamed of being a movie star. Just as he enjoyed reading *Superman* but never felt the urge to be the man who drew the comic book, Lenny liked the movies, but didn't have the slightest desire to act in one.

Performing for a camera and a roll of film was not what Lenny wanted at all. He needed a real audience: live, in-the-flesh people responding loudly, immediately, with laughter and applause that would warm his blood.

Lenny had wanted to be a comedian for almost as long as he could remember; even since before the war. He couldn't remember a whole lot about the way things were before his father went off to fight Hitler and Hirohito—not even, he realized sadly, much about his father.

But Lenny did remember the exact moment when he knew he wanted to be a comedian.

The summer before the war started, Lenny and Rozzie and their parents spent a week's vacation at Kaufman's Kountry Kottages, up in the mountains. They'd been going there every summer for several years. There was a lake nearby, in which Lenny and Rozzie hardly ever swam, because their mother was afraid of polio. There were woods with berries to pick, but Mrs. Kandell was convinced that the only berries to be found were the ones growing on the poison ivy.

So a good part of their week in the country was spent sitting on wooden chairs on the front porch of their Kottage, taking deep breaths of the fresh mountain air and talking about how much cooler it was here than in the city.

The last night of vacation, Lenny's father announced that he had a surprise for everyone. He made them get all dressed up in the best clothes they'd brought, then herded them into Mr. Kaufman's station wagon.

It was already past Lenny's bedtime when they set out along the dark, winding mountain road. Mysterious and exciting though the adventure promised to be, Lenny's eyelids were drooping as the station wagon stopped in front of one of the big, expensive resort hotels that dotted the Catskills.

"Everybody out," Lenny's father said. "The show is about to begin."

"Oh boy!" Rozzie started jumping up and down and shrieking with delight, but Lenny still didn't know what was going on and he was getting sleepier and sleepier.

The next thing he knew, they were in a darkened room with a lot of tables and a lot of people. A band was playing and a woman in a shimmering red dress was standing in a circle of light singing "Some of These Days."

After she finished singing, Lenny and Rozzie sipped at glasses of soda with lots of cracked ice in them, and a man and a woman in tight black costumes did a dance. The man picked the woman up and spun her around a lot, which Lenny thought was pretty good. Everybody clapped loudly when the dance was finished. Lenny clapped too. He wondered if maybe they'd have clowns or acrobats in the show. Whatever they had, Lenny knew he would like it better than sitting on the front porch counting fireflies.

There was a short pause, and Lenny and Rozzie had some more soda. Then the lights went down again. The spotlight hit the stage, and a young man in a snow-white tuxedo came bounding into the pool of light and began talking very fast.

Every once in a while he would have to stop, because people were laughing so hard you couldn't hear his words.

Fascinated, Lenny got to his knees on the chair and leaned forward so he could see better. He wasn't the least bit sleepy now. His eyes were wide open, and he couldn't take them off the man in the dazzling white suit.

The man was telling jokes, Lenny realized, and even though he didn't understand a lot of them, Lenny began to laugh when everyone else did. The man was funny—even if Lenny didn't know what a lot of the jokes meant, the man was still funny. He made his eyes and mouth do funny things, and fooled around with the microphone and joked with the musicians. When he did that, the drummer would do a little drumroll, and hit the cymbal to point up the joke. It was as if even the drums appreciated a good laugh, and that was how they laughed.

Near the end of the performance, when the comedian was really going strong and the laughs were coming one on top of the other like waves building and rolling and splashing against the shore, Lenny heard his mother's soprano giggle, trilling upward till it seemed louder than anyone else's.

Surprised, Lenny wanted to turn and look at her, just for a moment. His mother didn't laugh very often—not even back then, before his father went off to war. She worried so much—about polio and poison ivy and money—that a lot of the time she had little pinched lines between her eyes and not very many smiles on her lips.

Hearing her laugh this long and this hard was so unusual that Lenny finally managed to tear his attention away from the comedian and turn toward his mother.

He would never forget what he saw. She was

dabbing at her eyes with a little white handkerchief. She'd laughed so hard she was crying. She reached over her drink and laid her hand on Lenny's father's. He grinned, and she gazed up at him with a look Lenny had never seen in her eyes. He'd seen her angry, he'd seen her sad, and, of course, he'd seen her smile and be cheerful at least once in a while.

But he'd never seen her look like this: as if her eyes were *talking*, as if they were saying, perfectly clearly, "I love you. I'm happy. Thank you for that." And then his mother and father squeezed hands and Lenny, awed, turned back to watch the comedian finish his act.

The applause was thunderous. The cheers and yells filled the room and bounced off the walls. Lenny jumped up and down on his chair and clapped till his hands hurt.

And he knew, in that instant, there was nothing he wanted more than to be that man in that white suit, making everybody so happy that they loved one another, and loved him because he could make them feel that way.

There was a long line of kids in front of the ticket booth when they reached the theater. Lenny and Artie took their places at the end.

"I hope we can still get in," Artie said nervously. "I hope we can get seats together."

Lenny hoped so too. Half the fun of going to

the movies was sitting with Artie, talking back to the actors on the screen and making sarcastic remarks about the movie if it had a lot of mushy stuff in it.

The line seemed to move at a snail's pace toward the ticket booth.

"We're going to miss the cartoon," Artie fretted. "And it's a Bugs Bunny."

They finally reached the little glass box, where the woman snapped out their tickets. They followed the clusters of boisterous, shoving children into the darkened theater.

"Oh no, it did start already!" Artie wailed.

"It's only the coming attractions," Lenny assured him.

The children's section was jammed. Whatever the matron was supposed to be doing, she didn't seem to be doing it. She didn't seem to be doing anything. She just stood there, in her white uniform and black sweater, arms folded across her chest, looking sourly at the screen.

The kids were talking and giggling and crackling candy wrappers, paying no attention to the coming attractions, except for when they showed Danny Kaye kissing Virginia Mayo. Then they whistled and booed and made throwing-up noises.

Lenny and Artie peered around in the semi-darkness, looking for two seats together. The matron had a flashlight, but she never showed you a seat like the ushers did with the grown-ups. She just used her flashlight to single out kids who got too rowdy during the movie.

"Hey, there's a couple!" Lenny pointed. "Look, down there. Let's get 'em." They sprinted down the aisle to the row with the empty seats in the middle. They had to struggle over eight pairs of knees to get to them. Lenny stepped on a foot, and somebody kicked him in the ankle. The last boy he climbed over stuck his foot out and tripped him.

Lenny grabbed for the arm of an empty seat, missed, and suddenly found himself half sprawled across the girl in the next seat.

"Ouch!" she squealed.

"I'm sorry. Did you see what that rat did? He tripped me. On purpose." Lenny turned to look at him. "What'd you do that for?"

For some reason, Artie was huddled in his seat with his jacket collar pulled high up over his ears.

"Aw, shaddup," the rat growled. "The cartoon's on."

"Would you let go of my leg?" the girl said. "Would you get off me, please?"

Lenny gulped. He knew that voice.

He let go of the knee he'd been clutching as if his fingers were burning, then slumped into his seat. "Oh murder," he said under his breath.

"Is that you, Lenny?"

"Yeah. Hi, Georgina."

"I thought I recognized your voice."

He turned sideways to look at her. Bugs Bunny was just coming on, but she wasn't looking at the screen. She was looking sideways at *him*.

Lenny gulped again. He cleared his throat. "Sorry if I hurt you. But a funny thing happened on my way to the theater—"

"Shh!" Georgina popped a Jujyfruit into her mouth and turned away.

Lenny watched her watching the cartoon. Her jaw moved rhythmically as she chewed on the candy.

For a few minutes Georgina didn't take her eyes off Bugs Bunny and Lenny didn't take his eyes off Georgina. Her soft, long curls jiggled slightly as she shook the candy box to get the last few pieces out.

Without taking her eyes from the screen she held the box toward Lenny. "Want one?"

"Thanks." He took the next-to-the-last Jujyfruit out of the box. Unfortunately, it was green, but somehow Lenny didn't mind as much as he ordinarily would. He even sucked on it first before biting into it, to make it last longer. He watched the end of the cartoon intently.

The newsreel had a feature about summer fashions. When the models paraded around in sunsuits and shorts, some of the boys started to hoot and whistle. If Lenny hadn't been

sitting next to Georgina, he would probably
have yelled, "Hubba hubba!" and jabbed Artie
with his elbow. He might even have dared to
shoot a piece of popcorn at one of the bathing
beauties, hoping to hit some really interesting
part of her anatomy.

But he didn't have any popcorn, and for
some mysterious reason, Artie was still
scrunched down in his seat with his jacket over
his ears, and Lenny didn't think Georgina
would particularly appreciate being jabbed
with his elbow.

The next part of the newsreel was about the
postwar "House of the Future." A lady in an
apron was strolling around a gleaming white
kitchen, showing how easy it was to make
dinner with her modern appliances.

"I'm going for popcorn," Artie whispered.

Lenny glanced in his direction. The boy
who'd tripped him was gone. Artie's jacket
collar was back down on his neck and he was
already stumbling over legs toward the aisle.

"Okay, but hurry up!" Lenny called.
"You'll miss the serial!"

Nobody shushed him. Nobody was very interested in the Kitchen of the Future.

The serial was another matter entirely.

Everyone quieted down for that because it
was usually really exciting and full of action.
They showed one episode a week, and at the
end, the hero was always in some kind of awful

danger, almost definitely given up for dead in a plane crash or explosion or avalanche or something.

You couldn't imagine how he could possibly get out of the disaster alive, but he always did—at the beginning of the following week's installment. Then everyone watched breathlessly as he barreled through another fifteen minutes of hair-raising adventures, until the end of the chapter, when he once again faced certain death, and you were left in suspense until the *next* week to find out how he got out of *that* predicament.

The newsreel ended. Lenny looked around anxiously.

The serial was about to begin, and there was no sign of Artie. He'd miss the whole beginning if he didn't hurry up.

There was a summary of the previous action at the start of each chapter, so even as the letters LOST CITY OF THE JUNGLE flashed onto the screen, Lenny figured Artie still had a couple of minutes to make it back before this week's episode really began.

Everybody read the captions describing the characters, out loud, cheering at the picture of Rod Stanton and booing and hissing at the picture of Sir Eric Hazarius (alias Geoffrey London).

The plot summary was almost over. Lenny craned his neck to look for Artie. He didn't see him. But pushing his way down the row of seats from Georgina's side was the rat who had tripped him. He was carrying a bag of popcorn and had his jacket bunched up against his stomach.

Georgina tucked her knees sideways to let him pass.

Without thinking twice about it—without thinking about it at all, except for a fleeting notion of justice and revenge, which Rod Stanton would have understood—Lenny stuck his foot out.

Lenny got him in mid-stride, right between the ankles. The boy's back knee buckled and he flailed his arms wildly, trying to get his balance.

The popcorn shot straight up in the air, his jacket went sailing over two rows of heads, and Georgina shrieked and jumped out of her seat as a paper cup of soda he'd been sneaking in landed in her lap. The boy grabbed at a seat to keep himself from falling and knocked somebody in the back of the neck. That kid yelled, "Ow! Why'd you hit me?" and leaped out of his seat, ready to dive into Lenny's row after his attacker.

Lenny leaned forward. "Have a nice trip?" he asked pleasantly.

"You big ox! You spilled soda all over me!" Georgina cried.

Lenny yanked his foot back. He'd had no idea that the big ox was trying to sneak soda in, and he'd certainly never meant to hurt Georgina.

"He tripped me!" the boy roared. "That crudcake tripped me!"

"Look at my dress!" Georgina wailed. "It's ruined. You ruined it! And I've got soda all over me!"

By this time, the kids in the nearby rows were yelling at them to shut up, because the serial had started; the kids who couldn't see the commotion were yelling shut up at the kids who were yelling shut up, because they couldn't hear anything going on onscreen.

Kids started pelting the boy with popcorn and screaming for him to sit down.

"It's his fault! He tripped me!" The boy took a wild swing at Lenny. Lenny ducked, slithering down off his seat and onto the floor.

He heard a smack and a yelp of pain, and then, from the row behind, "Hey, what'd you punch me for? I didn't do anything to you!"

"Lenny Kandell, it's all your fault!" Georgina cried. "If you tripped him, it's all your fault." She leaned down to yell at him. "My dress is ruined and I'm all wet and now I have to go home and you're a *big dope!*"

She was practically in tears as she pushed her way past the boy, who was now sprawled

halfway into the next row. She stepped over Lenny and stumbled down the row to the center aisle.

By this time the matron's flashlight was singling out the cause of all the commotion. It zeroed in on the big ox's rear end, which stuck up over the top of the seat while the rest of him hung down over the back of it.

The two kids he'd hit were pointing at him and screaming, "He socked me! He socked me!" The air was thick with flying popcorn, and the entire children's section was yelling, "Shut up!" at each other.

Lenny crawled under Georgia's vacant seat and pulled it down so he was hidden. He chuckled softly. He was sorry about ruining Georgina's dress, but the matron was now ordering the ox out of the theater. Just what he deserved. And he was going. Yelling, complaining, being pelted with popcorn, but going.

Lenny's thirst for justice—and revenge—was satisfied.

The last thing he heard was a low growl from above him. "Lenny Kandell, eh? I'll get you for this, Lenny Kandell. I'll get you."

Things quieted down quickly after that, and within a few minutes Lenny figured it was safe to come out from under the seat.

He sat down with a little sigh of satisfaction and settled back to watch the end of the serial. There wasn't much left of it. Artie had returned to his seat and was holding a bag of popcorn.

"Boy, what you missed," Lenny whispered gleefully. "You should have seen it."

"I did see it." Artie sounded glum. "I was standing in the back. I saw the whole thing. Did you really trip him?"

"Heh heh heh," Lenny chuckled. "Heh heh heh."

"You shouldn't have."

"He tripped me," Lenny said indignantly. "He started it."

"Don't you know who that was?" Artie hissed. "You must be out of your mind."

"No, I don't know who it was. Who was it?"

"Mousie Blatner."

"Mousie Blatner? Who's Mousie Blatner?"

"Who's Mousie Blatner?" Artie groaned. "Who's Mousie Blatner? *He's notorious.*"

"Notorious?"

"Famous in a bad way," Artie explained.

"I know what *notorious* means!" Lenny said impatiently. "What's he notorious for?"

Artie told him, in a voice bleak with despair:

"He kills people."

SIX

THERE WERE TWO THINGS LENNY especially hated to do. One was going down to the basement to get the laundry out of the washing machine. The other was going up to the roof to hang the laundry out to dry.

It wasn't just because doing the wash was what they called woman's work, although that's how he complained to his mother whenever she asked him to do it. The truth was that the basement was a pretty scary place.

When you got out of the elevator, you had to walk down a long, gray corridor with concrete walls, past the boiler room, behind the stairs, past a dark, cavelike storage area to the dimly lit laundry room. It was an underground world of gloom and shadows, and the mysterious, ever-lurking presence of shapeless menace.

Sometimes, Lenny would pass the boiler room, and the furnace door would be open. He'd see Bill, the super, shoveling coal into the mouth of the furnace, feeding the roaring blaze, and Lenny would feel a blast of heat surge out of the room. Crazy shadows slithered and leaped around the walls, and Bill was a hunched silhouette, outlined in flame.

To Lenny, peering into the boiler room was like catching a glimpse of Hell.

Lenny's imagination ran wild in the basement. There was no telling who—or *what*—might be creeping down the dark corridor or lying in wait behind the stairs.

If he got out of the basement alive, Lenny still had to haul the heavy load of wet wash up to the roof and hang it on the line. There were two problems with that.

Lenny didn't want anyone to spot him doing something as sissy as hanging up wash, so once he was safely on the elevator, he would begin worrying that one of the kids would see him and start razzing him. The other problem was that Lenny was really too short to reach the clothesline. He had to stand on his toes and stretch; by the time he finished hanging up a whole load of wash, his shoulders ached and his toes felt like they were permanently bent in the wrong direction.

Sometimes there was an old box or crate

around that Lenny could stand on, but he had to keep climbing on and off the box every time he hung something up, and it got to be a real pain.

The day after the movies, Lenny had to hang up the wash; scary as the trip to the basement was ordinarily, it was ten times worse that Sunday.

Lenny could not stop thinking of what Artie had told him about Mousie Blatner.

Their urgent, whispered conversation had taken up the last part of the serial and a good fifteen minutes of the first feature.

"You don't really mean he *kills* people, you just mean—" Lenny stopped. He couldn't think what else Artie could mean.

"He kills people," Artie insisted. "He killed a kid just for calling him Maurice. He pushed him off a roof."

"Why'd the kid call him Maurice?"

"That's his name. But he doesn't let anyone call him that. Only Mousie."

Lenny didn't think "Mousie" was such a great name, but maybe compared to Maurice . . .

"Well, then how come he isn't in jail?"

"I don't know. Maybe they couldn't prove he did it."

"Then how do you know he did?"

"Everybody knows. And he killed a kid once over a comic book. Strangled him with his bare hands."

"Aw, baloney," Lenny said nervously. "Why'd he do that?"

"He wanted the comic book."

Lenny suddenly felt as if his spine had dissolved and he would slither down off the seat and onto the floor again. "I don't believe it!"

"Shh! Shut up, will ya?" Two kids in the front of them turned around briefly.

Artie bent his head closer to Lenny's. "Swear to God."

"Hope to die?" Lenny whispered.

"Hope to die. Hope my tongue turns black and my teeth rot and my fingernails fall out."

Lenny groaned softly. After a swear like that, how could he doubt that Artie was telling the truth? Lenny didn't notice much of what was happening on the screen after that. He kept thinking about what it would feel like to be strangled by Mousie Blatner's bare hands. Then he kept trying *not* to think about what it would feel like.

"Hey, Artie, let's see *Spook Busters* again."

"I have to go home."

"Aw, come on, don't you want to see it one more time?"

"We'd have to sit through the whole show all over again."

"Yeah, I know," Lenny said. That was the

whole idea. If Mousie Blatner was hanging around the theater wanting to "get" Lenny, he certainly wouldn't wait through another whole show. That would be almost three-and-a-half hours. He'd figure that Lenny had managed to sneak by him when the first show let out, and he'd just give up waiting and go home.

"Say, Artie, I wonder what's the most number of shows anybody ever sat through?"

"I have to go *home*," Artie insisted.

"We could maybe set a world's record for the most number of shows anybody ever—"

"I promised my mother I'd come home right after the show."

"You didn't say which one!"

"Look, I'll tell you what," Artie offered, "I'll go outside and reconnoiter." *Reconnoiter* was not one of Artie's *Reader's Digest* words. He'd learned it from war movies, so Lenny knew what it meant. "You wait in the lobby, and if the coast is clear I'll come back and signal you."

Lenny was a little embarrassed that Artie had caught on so fast to why he'd wanted to stay in the movies. But after all, it was Artie who'd told him how dangerous Mousie Blatner was. Artie of all people would understand if Lenny was a little nervous about the prospect of running into an enraged killer.

Lenny reluctantly hauled himself out of his seat and followed Artie down the aisle. "Well, look," he began, trying to make his voice sound cheerful, "he just said he'd *get* me. He didn't say he was going to *kill* me."

"I think that *get* and *kill* are probably . . . uh . . . synonymous to Mousie."

"What?"

"They mean the same thing."

"Oh murder," Lenny muttered.

"Exactly."

Lenny waited in the lobby, hands in his pockets, trying to look nonchalant. Artie promised to walk around the whole block to make sure Mousie wasn't lurking in any doorways, so it was several minutes before he came back and flashed Lenny a thumbs-up sign.

Lenny took a deep breath and walked out onto the sidewalk.

He wished he had his pocketknife with him.

All week he'd kept it in his desk drawer, just taking it out to stroke and admire several times a day. But he never walked out of his room with it—not after what had happened with Aunt Harriet's fur. He pulled the various blades out, first one by one, then all together, but he didn't really know what else he could do with it. He plucked a hair from his head and tried to slash through it with the knife, sneaked a can of peas and carrots into his room and attempted to use the can opener attachment, but after that, he was at a loss.

I sure could use it now, Lenny thought. If

Mousie Blatner came at him, all Lenny would have to do would be to brandish the knife, and old Mousie would take off like a scared rabbit. It would be self-defense. Lenny wouldn't have to actually use the knife, he was sure of that. He'd simply wave it in front of Mousie.

But the knife was home in his desk drawer, where it was doing him no good at all, except keeping his promise to his mother. And a fat lot she'd care about promises after Lenny was dead.

Lenny talked very fast all the way home, hoping Artie wouldn't notice that he was looking over his shoulder every two minutes.

" '. . . thinks he's a refrigerator. That's terrible!' 'You're telling me, Doctor. He sleeps with his mouth open and the little light keeps me awake. . . . You think that's bad? My sister thinks she's a chicken. She runs around the house scratching and clucking and trying to build a nest.' 'That's certainly peculiar. What are you doing about it?' 'Nothing—with prices the way they are, we can use the eggs. . . .' "

Artie chuckled appreciatively all the way home; but Lenny saw that even Artie couldn't help looking over his shoulder a few times before they got to their building.

When the elevator stopped at the third floor and Lenny started to get off, Artie suddenly grabbed his hand and shook it hard. "So long . . . pal," he said huskily.

Lenny wished he hadn't made it sound so *final*.

Now, tiptoeing down the dark hall to the laundry room, Lenny had even more to worry about than the imaginary creatures that huddled under the stairs.

What if Mousie Blatner had followed him home yesterday? What if *Mousie Blatner* was hiding under the stairs, just waiting to catch Lenny alone? Maybe Mousie didn't "get" him yesterday because Artie was there. Maybe Mousie wanted to kill him when there'd be no witnesses.

Lenny stuck his hand into his pocket and felt for his knife. It was comforting to hold on to it as he crept around the stairs, then dashed past the storeroom and into the laundry room.

He pulled the wash out of the machine, standing sideways so he could keep an eye on the laundry room door. Carrying the pocketknife with him was not really breaking his promise, because he wasn't taking it out of the house. The basement was part of the house, the roof was part of the house, so technically he was still keeping his word.

In any case, this could very well be a matter of life and death, and in a matter of life and death, you were entitled to do almost anything that would help you come out alive.

Unfortunately, making his way back to the

elevator with the basket of wet laundry, Lenny couldn't keep his hand on the knife. The basket was too heavy and bulky to carry with one hand. He thought briefly of carrying the knife between his teeth, but that was risky. A neighbor might see him and tell his mother that Lenny was running around the building with a knife in his mouth. And if Mousie Blatner didn't kill him, there was a distinct possibility that his mother would.

Lenny put the basket down and punched the button for the elevator. He reached into his pocket and clutched the knife. My father, he told himself, wouldn't be afraid—not of the basement, not even of Mousie Blatner. Thinking about his father helped a little.

Lenny straightened up, squared his shoulders, took a deep breath, and waited for the elevator to reach the basement.

He heard it coming down from the first floor and stood to one side so that if anyone happened to be in the elevator, Lenny would see him before he saw Lenny.

The door slid open. Lenny waited a moment, to make sure no one was there, then picked up the basket. Suddenly, from somewhere down the dark corridor, he heard a clank and a thud.

Lenny shrieked.

Like a shot, he plunged for the elevator. He smashed the row of buttons with his elbow, not caring which one he hit, just knowing that any one of them would make the door close and the elevator start upward.

He dropped the basket and reached for his knife. The door snicked closed and the elevator began to move.

Lenny leaned against the wall of the car, gasping for breath. His palms were so damp the knife slipped around in his fingers when he tried to get a grip on it.

He felt the elevator slowing, and realized he'd pushed so many buttons it might very well stop on every floor before he got to six.

He took a deep breath and tried to get hold of himself.

No matter how startled he'd been, he couldn't stay jumpy like this. That thud and clunk had probably been Bill with his toolbox. Lenny had to be prepared, to be calm and alert every time the elevator door slid open. Because if Mousie Blatner hadn't been in the basement, he could be waiting to spring into the elevator and onto Lenny at any floor between the basement and the roof.

The elevator stopped on the first floor, but no one was waiting. It stopped on the second floor. Mrs. Fidler, the deaf old lady from 2B, squinted at Lenny as the door opened.

"Down?" she shouted. Without waiting for him to answer, she stepped into the elevator, pulling her little dachshund in behind her. "Sit, Fritzi!"

Lenny pushed the button for six, relieved that Mrs. Fidler would be in the elevator with him all the way up. Then he pushed the button for the first floor.

"Oh, up," Mrs. Fidler said. She looked at the basket of wash and nodded her head. "You're a good boy, helping out your poor mother!" she shouted.

Mrs. Fidler always yelled, because being deaf, she didn't know how loud she talked. This time Lenny didn't mind. If Mousie Blatner wanted to get him when there were no witnesses around, old Mrs. Fidler was perfectly good protection. He didn't even mind when Fritzi began chewing on his sneaker laces.

"Sit, Fritzi!" Mrs. Fidler yanked the leash. Fritzi sat down and chewed on his sneaker laces.

By the time they reached the sixth floor, Lenny was a lot calmer. He hauled the wash out of the elevator and staggered up the flight of stairs to the iron door that led out to the roof. He balanced the basket on his knee and slowly, warily pushed the door open.

SEVEN

As far as Lenny could see, there was nothing on the roof but a clothesline of white shirts, their sleeves flapping in the breeze.

Lenny carried the basket of clothes over to the washlines and put it down. It was a beautiful, clear day, and Lenny was in no hurry to get the job done and return to the apartment. Uncle Joe and Aunt Harriet might be there. As if he didn't have enough on his mind, with Mousie Blatner planning to kill him, Lenny still had to worry about paying for the cleaning and/or repairing of Aunt Harriet's stoned marten.

How much, he thought, can one person put up with? It hardly seemed fair that a kid like him should have so many problems all at the same time.

Lenny wandered over to the edge of the roof. There was a brick ledge just higher than his waist, and he leaned on it and looked out over the city. All of New York was spread out before him, and the view was exhilarating. From the roof you didn't see any of the ugly parts—just a vast, beautiful cityscape, with the skyscrapers of Manhattan shimmering in the sunlight.

Once, when he was very little, Lenny and his father were on the roof, and his father had picked him up in his arms and said, "Look, you can see the Empire State Building from here." At the time, Lenny was so young he didn't even know what the Empire State Building was. But now, whenever Lenny went up to the roof, he stood right where his father had held him and peered into the distance till his eyes picked out the spire of the tallest building in the world.

Lenny gripped the ledge and fought the familiar urge to look down at the sidewalk. He loved to look out across the rooftops, but he hated to look down at the street six stories below. Something mysterious and scary happened to him when he looked down.

First he would think how horrible it would be to fall off the roof and plunge six floors to the sidewalk, and that would make him shudder. But then, he'd suddenly find himself wondering what it would feel like to jump off the roof, to go sailing over the edge of the building, hurtling down, down . . .

This made Lenny dizzy with terror. He couldn't understand why one part of him seemed to feel such a disturbing, irresistible urge to do something that only a crazy person would do. When the dizziness overcame him, he would tear himself away from the edge of the roof, walking a good distance away from it, as if the urge would become overpowering if he stood there looking down one moment longer.

Lenny looked, very briefly, because he couldn't help it, but almost immediately he forced himself to back away and move toward the clotheslines. He wondered, as he always did, if this dark, confusing impulse meant that he was crazy.

Lenny sighed and reached down for a sheet to hang up. There was a bag of clothespins hanging on the line. He tugged at it and pulled it off. He jumped to grab the clothesline and tried to throw the sheet over it with one hand. He went around to the other side and tugged, trying to make the sheet hang more evenly. The breeze picked it up and lapped it against his face. He pushed it away, irritably, and jammed a couple of clothespins over it.

Lenny saw there was another sheet to hang up and groaned. He looked around and spotted a wooden crate on one side of the stairwell. He brought it over to the clothesline and stood on it to hang up the second sheet.

When both sheets were hanging fairly smoothly, Lenny got down off the box and went to pull the laundry basket down to the next spot on the line. He bent down, and suddenly noticed that the two sheets, hanging side by side with a little gap between them, looked like . . . curtains. On a stage.

Lenny spread the sheets apart and stuck his head between them. "Ta daa! Ladies and gentlemen, your favorite and mine, star of stage, screen, and radio, the incomparable, the hilarious—LENNY DELL!"

"Yay!" Lenny cheered, and pushing the sheets apart, he stepped through the gap so he was in front of them, then bowed.

"Thank you, thank you very much ladies and gentlemen, you're very kind. I want to tell you, a funny thing—"

A sudden brainstorm made him interrupt himself. He hauled the wooden Elmhurst Dairy milk crate in front of the sheets and stood on it.

Just like a stage! He was still holding a clothespin in his hand, and he brought it up to his mouth like a microphone.

"I was doing a show in Buffalo the other night and I don't know anyone in Buffalo, so I was feeling a little lonely and blue. I went into this restaurant and asked the waitress for some fried eggs and a kind word. She brought me the eggs and started to walk away and I said, 'Hey, how about the kind word?' And she leaned down and whispered, 'Don't eat the eggs.'

"Listen, you think that's bad? My kid has such rotten table manners, he's always reaching for things. I keep telling him to ask people to please pass the plate, but no, he keeps reaching for whatever he wants. Finally the other night I got fed up. 'Hey, sonny,' I said, 'I wish you'd stop reaching for everything. Haven't you got a tongue?' And he said, 'Yeah, but my arm's longer.' "

The sun shone on Lenny like a spotlight, and he could almost see the rows and rows of seats stretching around the whole roof, hundreds of laughing faces, all looking up at him with admiration and anticipation.

Lenny waited for the laughter to die down a little.

"But my mother-in-law, she's really something. Nothing throws her. She went to the doctor because she kept getting these terrible earaches. The doctor looked at her ear and found a little piece of string dangling from it. So he started to pull on it. And he pulled, and pulled, and the string got longer and longer. And finally he gave a good, hard yank and a big bouquet of flowers fell out of her ear. 'Good Lord,' the doctor says, 'where did these flowers come from?' And my mother-in-law says, 'How should I know? Isn't there a card?' "

"Thank you, thank you, you're a wonderful audience." Lenny tried to quiet them down.

"Wait, that's nothing. This woman, nothing throws her, nothing impresses her either. She went on a trip to the Grand Canyon, and there was this daredevil stuntman who was going to try and ride a unicycle across a tightrope stretched over the Grand Canyon, while he was blindfolded. And while he was riding the unicycle he was going to play 'Humoresque' on the violin.

"So my mother-in-law and father-in-law stood there and watched as they blindfolded this fellow, and he got on the unicycle, stuck the violin under his chin, and started pedaling along this tightrope right over the Grand Canyon, fiddling all the while.

"And my father-in-law turns to my mother-in-law and says, 'Isn't that incredible? Isn't that terrific? Come on, Edna, even *you* have to admit he's amazing.'

"And my mother-in-law shrugs and says, 'He's okay—but he's no Heifetz.' "

For a change of pace, Lenny did a couple of songs, which the audience loved. They were always surprised when such a funny comedian could sing a love song like "I Don't Want to Walk without You" with real emotion.

Lenny went on with his act and forgot everything—the basket of cold, soggy laundry, the Empire State Building, the basement, Mousie Blatner, Aunt Harriet and her fur stole, Miss Randolph and *Hiawatha,* his mother . . .

There were only Lenny and his jokes, Lenny and his songs, Lenny and his audience. Lenny Dell was on stage, and when Lenny Dell was on stage, Lenny Kandell's problems were dim, distant shadows, with no more substance than the phantoms that dwelt under the basement stairs.

It was much later when Lenny finally finished hanging up the wash.

He was just about to go downstairs when a stiff gust of wind whipped the shirts on the next clothesline and a damp, flapping sleeve smacked across Lenny's cheek.

He swatted at the sleeve with his hand and leaped back.

"Slap me, will you? Scoundrel! Cad! Poltroon!" He watched the shirt dance on the line for a moment, and his eyes lit up. Grinning broadly, he dug into his pocket for his knife.

"I challenge you to ze duel!" He pulled the knife open and held it out like a sword. He raised his other arm in a fencing position and charged the shirt. *"En garde!"*

"Swish! Swoosh!" He made elaborate circles and figure eights in the air with the knife, leaping forward and backward like one of the Three Musketeers.

The breeze blew the shirt away from Lenny. "Coward!" Lenny taunted. "Poltroon! Come on and fight like a man, you shirt!" He chuckled to himself.

He dove forward, making a great, swooping arc with the knife, just as the wind blew the shirt back toward him. Before Lenny could stop the momentum of his arm, the knife slashed clear down the front of the shirt.

Lenny heard a short, sharp *ri . . . ip . . . p,* then six little plips as the white buttons hit the roof and rolled off in different directions, like a broken string of pearls.

The knife dropped from Lenny's numb fingers with a thunk.

Oh murder.

Lenny began to run around looking for the buttons, till he realized that even if he found them, there was nothing he could do with them but stick them in the shirt pocket or throw them away. He thought maybe he'd better look at the shirt, to see what the ripping sound had been. Reluctantly, he walked back to the line. I can't look, he thought. I just can't look.

I *have* to look. With a great effort of will, he forced himself to look up at the shirt. It was hanging open now, with all the front buttons gone but one. That one was dangling by a thread, and there was a whole line of little holes above it where the other buttons had been. The back of the shirt was flapping in two separate directions; it had been slit right down the middle.

Lenny clapped his hands over his eyes. *What am I gonna do?*

Maybe I'm dreaming, he thought. Maybe this is a nightmare. Maybe when I open my eyes the shirt will be in one piece and all the buttons will be back on it and I'll have imagined the whole thing.

Cautiously, Lenny opened his eyes.

He wasn't dreaming.

What was he going to do?

There was only, Lenny realized, one possible thing to do. He reached up and pulled the shirt off the line. He stuck the clothespins in his pocket, so it wouldn't be obvious that something had been hanging there. He wandered over to the far edge of the roof, overlooking the back courtyard of the apartment building.

He looked around furtively, then forced himself to glance down. The courtyard was empty. Lenny pitched the shirt over the edge of the roof, and didn't even wait to watch it swoop and flutter to the ground.

He didn't know whose laundry it was. It could have belonged to anyone in the building. All he could do was hope that whoever had

hung up that load of wash didn't count the shirts.

He bent down and picked up his knife. He folded the blade back in and stuck it in his pocket. This knife, which Uncle Joe said couldn't stab anything, had mutilated a fur stole and a dress shirt in one week. This knife, which he'd wanted so badly, was causing him more trouble . . .

Maybe he'd better put the knife back in his desk drawer and forget about it for a while.

"Stupid knife," Lenny muttered. "Stupid, dumb knife . . ."

EIGHT

"Hey, Miss Randolph, do you know the weather report for Mexico?"

"Chili today and hot tamale. Take your seat, Leonard."

"Darn."

But Lenny didn't really care. He was in high spirits this morning.

Aunt Harriet had come down with the grippe, so she and Uncle Joe had missed yesterday's visit. Lenny and Artie had spent the afternoon listening to the Dodger game on the radio, and the Dodgers had won. Nobody had come to accuse Lenny of assaulting a shirt. And best of all, Mousie Blatner hadn't killed him on the way to school.

For once, Lenny didn't mind sitting in the stuffy classroom with the drab green walls.

Mousie Blatner would never try anything on school grounds, not if he didn't want hundreds of witnesses. The way Lenny figured it, he didn't have a worry in the world—at least, not until three o'clock.

He didn't even mind that Georgina Schultz acted cold and stuck-up and made sure their shoulders didn't touch when they had reading. When Miss Randolph called on her, Lenny noticed how the tip of Georgina's tongue flicked around the edge of her lips before she started to read.

Someday he would explain it all to her. He wasn't sure how, but he was sure she would understand.

"Oh, Lenny," he could hear her say, "what does a little stain on a dress matter compared to the terrible danger you were in? And it's all my fault. If I hadn't yelled at you, Mousie Blatner would never have known your name. It is all on account of me that you faced death."

"Think nothing of it," Lenny would say gallantly. "I would gladly face death for you, Georgina . . ."

Georgina handed him the reader. Miss Randolph had called on him, and he didn't know what line they were up to. Sometimes Georgina would hold her finger under the line where he was supposed to start when she knew his mind had been wandering, but now she just shoved the book at him and turned her head away.

Lenny took a wild stab and started reading the first paragraph on the page.

"We've finished that part, Leonard," Miss Randolph said.

"Oh, yeah, but it was so good I thought I'd read it again," Lenny said.

A couple of the kids giggled. They were quickly silenced by Miss Randolph's narrowing eyes. "That won't be necessary. Begin where Georgina left off."

Wasn't she even going to give him a clue? For all Lenny knew, Georgina didn't have the book open to the right page when she handed it to him. Maybe she was so mad she deliberately turned back a few pages to get him in trouble.

Taking another blind guess, Lenny skipped two paragraphs and began again.

"We've read that part too, Leonard." Miss Randolph's voice was sharp.

"Am I getting warmer?" Lenny asked hopefully.

"You needn't waste our time any longer," Miss Randolph said. "You'll make up for your daydreaming during recess. Thomas, will you continue?"

Georgina snatched the reader back and shot him a smug little "so there" look. Lenny sighed. He wondered why he'd imagined that

Georgina would ever say anything nice to him. She'd probably cheer when Mousie Blatner rubbed him out.

Lenny was sorry that Miss Randolph was annoyed with him again, but he was not a bit disturbed about staying in during recess.

After all, Mousie could be searching the whole schoolyard for Lenny, and if he didn't see him out with all the other kids, he might figure Lenny went to a different school. By the time he'd cased all the other public schools in Flushing, Mousie would probably be mad at somebody else and would have completely forgotten that he'd wanted to kill Lenny in the first place.

So Lenny stayed in the classroom after lunch and read all the pages he was supposed to read that morning. He read them carefully, just in case Miss Randolph decided to check up on him with a test or some questions. He didn't even pay any attention to the shouts of the kids playing punchball or the shrill chanting of the girls jumping rope.

When he finished the chapter, Lenny put his chin in his hand and let his gaze drift toward the picture of George Washington in the front of the room. But he wasn't seeing George Washington; he was seeing Georgina Schultz, with her bouncy, golden curls and her little pink tongue flicking around the corners of her mouth.

If I bought her a new dress, Lenny thought dreamily, I bet she'd talk to me again. She wouldn't be mad at me anymore for ruining her dress if I got her a new one—a real expensive one.

"Oh, Lenny, you shouldn't have! Oh, this is too expensive. I never meant for you to buy me a new dress. This is much prettier than the one that got Coke spilled on it."

Yeah, that would do it all right, Lenny thought. Not only would Georgina forgive him, she'd be grateful to him. "Every time I wear it I'll think of you, Lenny . . ."

How much would a new dress cost? he wondered.

He sighed. He didn't even know if he'd have to pay for cleaning and/or sewing Aunt Harriet's stoned marten, or how much *that* would be; what was the use of dreaming about buying Georgina a new dress? Lenny began to think that money was the solution to all his problems.

If he were rich, he wouldn't be worrying about how much it cost to fix a fur stole; he'd be able to make up with Georgina; he'd even find a way to handle Mousie Blatner. He could hire a bodyguard, for instance, or go to Australia for a few months, or, if all else failed, bribe Mousie not to kill him.

Though Lenny liked to think of his father as

a war hero and told himself over and over again what a brave man he was, he had to admit that his father had not been particularly good at earning money.

Even before the war, the Kandells had never been what Mrs. Kandell called "comfortable." Since Lenny always had good food and shoes that fit, he figured that by "comfortable" his mother meant rich. Everybody his mother said was "comfortable" seemed to be rolling in money. Lenny sometimes wondered what she would call a millionaire.

Lenny's mother had always worried about money. As far back as Lenny could remember she talked about it constantly. Mr. Kandell was a shoe salesman, and Lenny's mother never seemed to get used to that. "Someone with your brains," she used to say, "selling shoes. It's a crime, that's what it is. Think what you could be today if you'd finished college. Look at your brother, Joe. He and Harriet aren't suffering any."

"Joe didn't go to college at all," Lenny's father would say.

"That's beside the point. They're very comfortable."

After Lenny's father enlisted in the army, Mrs. Kandell was more bitter than ever. Lenny could still remember her sitting with Aunt Harriet and Uncle Joe, crying, "Why? Why? How could he leave me like this, with two babies to take care of? He didn't have to go."

It bothered Lenny to hear his mother talk that way. He thought he knew what Uncle Joe meant when he tried to calm her down. "He felt he had to go, Ida. He had to do something about Hitler. He was doing it for you and the kids."

"For me and the kids he should have stayed home."

"He thought his country needed him."

"We needed him more."

Lenny had never thought they were poor, and if his mother hadn't talked so much about money, he probably wouldn't have noticed that there never seemed to be very much. Even after the war, when prices were high and his mother's job at Annette's paid so much less than what she'd earned in the factory while his father was in the service, Lenny didn't want so many things that he felt much need for money.

What he wanted most of all—to be a famous comedian—didn't cost any money. It just took hard work and talent. And the things he liked to do—listening to the radio, playing stickball, rehearsing his act, rooting for the Dodgers, and fooling around with Artie—didn't take any money either.

But now he had minus-ten cents to his name (he owned Rozzie a dime for the movies) and a bunch of problems that could be solved in a minute if he had some mazuma to spread around.

Lenny gazed at the picture of George Washington next to the blackboard.

And thought of dollar bills.

"You need a disguise," Artie said. "You looked pretty conspicious walking home with your jacket pulled over your head."

"What I need is some dough," Lenny said. "Besides, we made it home, didn't we? He didn't spot me, did he?"

Lenny flipped through Artie's *Red Ryder* comic book. "Say, Artie, do you know anyone who actually made money selling Cloverine Salve?"

"I don't even know what Cloverine Salve is," Artie said. "Although their ads are certainly ubiquitous."

"Yeah, well, they say you can make lots of money selling it. You think that's true?"

Artie shrugged.

"I have to think of some way to make money," Lenny said. "It's my only hope."

"You think money is a panacea?" Artie asked.

"I don't think it's Ipana seer," Lenny retorted. "I just think it'll solve all my problems. Now, come on, use your bean. How can I make a fast stash?"

"Rob a bank."

"Very funny. Come on, this is serious. Are you going to help me or not?"

"Okay, okay. Let's see. We could collect empty soda bottles. That's two cents a bottle when we turn them in."

"At that rate I'll be seventy-five before I have enough money. If Mousie lets me live that long."

Artie glanced at his *Captain Marvel* comic. "You could sell newspapers," he said. "Like Billy Batson."

"You think there's any money in it?"

"Probably not. If a paper costs only three cents, how much could you make?"

"Not much," Lenny said glumly.

"Hey, maybe you could go on one of those quiz shows!" Artie said. "You could win a lot of money on a quiz show."

"*You* could, maybe. I'm not smart enough for that."

"You could go on 'It Pays to Be Ignorant,' " Artie chuckled.

"Yock, yock, thanks a lot."

"Just kidding," Artie said. "Let's see. What about selling encyclopedias door to door? You'd probably be a good salesman. You could get your customers in a munificent mood with a joke or two—"

"Do you think they'd hire a kid?" Lenny asked dubiously. "I mean, you never hear of an encyclopedia sales*boy*."

"Well . . . I don't know. But I bet they make good money."

"I have a feeling they'd think I'm too young," Lenny said.

"I have a feeling I'm running out of ideas," Artie said.

For several minutes they sat in gloomy silence.

"Hey!" Artie said suddenly. "What about baby-sitting? Your sister makes a lot of money baby-sitting."

Lenny brightened up. "Yeah, she makes twenty-five cents an hour. Let's see, if I sat with a kid for four hours, I'd make a dollar. If I baby-sit every day for a week . . . seven dollars a week . . . twenty-eight dollars a month! Not bad. Hey, and if I could sit for three kids at once—that would be seventy-five cents an hour times four hours!"

A vivid picture began forming in Lenny's mind: stacks and stacks of quarters piled up, higher and higher, until they got so high they started to spill over in showers of silver. Lenny was so excited he leaped up and ran to Rozzie's desk for a piece of paper to figure on.

Behind him, he heard a braying laugh. He whirled around. Rozzie was standing in the doorway, holding her schoolbooks against her stomach and looking at Lenny.

At least Lenny assumed she was looking at him. She wore dark green sunglasses with white plastic frames, so he couldn't see her eyes, but her orangy-red lips were spread in a big, mocking grin.

"What's so funny?" Lenny demanded.

"The thought of anyone letting you baby-sit with their kid." Rozzie dropped her books on her bed and took off her sunglasses. "You're barely old enough to take care of yourself, let alone somebody else."

Lenny saw all those quarters he'd piled up in his imagination disappear in an instant, as if a giant hand had swooped down and snatched them all away.

He was suddenly so dejected that he didn't even notice the scorn in Rozzie's voice.

"You don't think people would trust me with their kids?"

"You're a *child*," Rozzie said. "I didn't start baby-sitting till I was thirteen." She leaned toward the mirror over her dresser and put on fresh lipstick, even though she didn't need it. She pressed a tissue between her lips to blot up the excess, but her mouth still looked like she'd smeared it with ketchup. She wet her pinky and stroked her eyebrows, then stood back a little to admire the effect.

"Careful you don't break the mirror," Lenny said dispiritedly. Ordinarily he would have reminded her not to look at a clock, because her face would make it stop—but he couldn't work up any enthusiasm for needling his sister.

"I'm going to Mimi's," she said. She slung her shoulder bag across her chest and picked up her sunglasses. "I'll be back in time to start supper."

She paused at the doorway and looked back at Lenny over her shoulder. "And when you make your first million, remember you owe me ten cents."

She was still cackling when the apartment door slammed shut behind her.

Artie looked up from *Captain Marvel,* which he'd been pretending to read while Rozzie was in the room. "Well, what now?"

"I don't know," Lenny said hopelessly. "It sounded like such a good idea."

"I've been thinking," Artie said.

"Yeah?" Lenny leaned forward eagerly.

"About your problem."

"Yeah, yeah?"

"And it seems to me that the only people who make a lot of money fast are movie stars and inventors. Somebody makes one movie and he can be an overnight success. Or a guy can invent something new and millions of people buy it and suddenly he's rich."

"So? What does that have to do with me?"

"Nothing. That's just my point. You're probably not going to come up with a brilliant invention in the foreseeable future, and you probably won't be a famous comedian for at least ten years, so the only thing you can do right now is collect soda bottles, sell newspapers, and wear a disguise."

"Oh, swell," Lenny said. "Just swell. And I thought you were on to something."

"I'm sorry," Artie said, "but I can't think of anything else. How can you be an overnight success if you haven't even had your first show yet?"

Lenny's mouth dropped open. He stared at Artie, his eyes wide. For a moment he sat rigid and unmoving, as if he were having some kind of attack.

"Hey, what's the matter?" Artie jumped up in alarm. "Lenny, what's with you?"

"That's it," Lenny breathed. "That's it!"

He could see it as clearly as he always did, the rows and rows of upturned faces, a sea of clapping hands, tears of laughter streaming down hundreds of cheeks.

But this time, something new: the tinkle of coins as they dropped, one after another, into a brimming cigar box . . .

"Artie," Lenny said, his eyes shining with vision, "Artie, you're a *genius!*"

NINE

WALKING TO SCHOOL THE NEXT day, wearing Rozzie's sunglasses and a fake handlebar mustache that Uncle Joe had given him, Lenny asked himself if his father would have resorted to a disguise if Mousie Blatner had been after *him*.

Well, if Lenny's father had fought in the jungles of the Philippines, he'd probably have had one of those camouflage outfits—the helmet that looked like plants and leaves and things, and a splotchy uniform that blended in with the trees and vines. A disguise was the same as camouflage, wasn't it? And if Lenny's father wore camouflage, there was certainly no reason for Lenny to feel ashamed about wearing it.

"Is anybody looking at me?" He asked nervously. "I can hardly see through these sunglasses." He'd sneaked them off Rozzie's dresser, and he hoped he'd be able to put them back before she got home. She'd probably kill him if she found out he'd filched them. But she'd have to wait in line.

"You're the cynosure of all eyes," Artie said.

"But *is anyone looking at me?*"

"Everyone is looking at you!" Artie said irritably. "And me."

"Do you think they recognize me?"

"They recognize me," Artie said. "This is embarrassing."

"You know, this could be a good publicity stunt," Lenny said. "Hey, that's it! I'll make a sign and wear it. Then everyone will think we're just doing it to call attention to the show."

"Not a bad idea," Artie grunted. "If we're going to be laughingstocks, it might as well be in a good cause."

Lenny thought staying alive was a pretty good cause, but he was too excited, thinking about the terrific sign he would make, to point that out.

They walked into the schoolyard and headed for their class line. Girls giggled and snickered as they walked by. A few made some smart remarks about Lenny's disguise, but it only bothered him when someone said, "Hey,

Lenny, what're you got up for? It ain't Halloween."

"They recognize me," Lenny said anxiously. "Artie, how come they recognize me? I thought this was such a good disguise."

Everyone started calling out to Lenny as they got in line. With so many kids pointing at him and saying his name and yelling wisecracks, Lenny started to get panicky. Mousie Blatner, if he was anywhere nearby, would be even more likely to spot him now.

Suddenly Artie said, "If you think this is funny, wait'll you see the show!"

"What show? Lenny, you having a show? Hey, can I come?" A whole bunch of kids clustered around Lenny and Artie and started peppering them with questions.

"This Sunday at two o'clock," Artie said. "On the roof of one-forty-one ten Franklin Avenue. Admission only ten cents, one thin dime, the tenth part of a dollar. Watch for our signs."

Out of the corner of his eye, Lenny saw that even Georgina was listening, leaning forward on the fringe of the crowd.

Lenny forgot for the moment about Mousie Blatner. He looked at Georgina, heard all the kids around him clamoring for more details about the show, and began to see all those dimes piling up in the cigar box.

You had to hand it to Artie. He really *was* a

genius. He'd even thought up the perfect thing
to put on the sign.

IF YOU THINK I'M FUNNY NOW
WAIT TILL YOU SEE MY SHOW!!
SUN. 2 PM 141-10 FRANKLIN AVE.
ON THE ROOF   10¢

Lenny spent the first part of the recess let-
tering the sign on a big piece of oak tag Miss
Randolph had let him use. He put the red and
black crayons back into the supply cabinet and
thanked Miss Randolph again for the oak tag.

Carrying the sign in one hand, he went down
the stairs and toward the side door leading to
the schoolyard. He paused to put on the fake
mustache and the sunglasses: he peered out at
the swarms of kids in the yard, wondering
where Mousie Blatner was. But just for a moment.

No, he told himself firmly. I am not going to
worry about Mousie Blatner now. My father
wouldn't be afraid to go out there, and neither
am I.

Besides, Mousie Blatner wouldn't dare do
anything with all those people crowding
around Lenny, trying to see the sign. Why,
Mousie probably wouldn't even be able to get
near him if he wanted to.

Holding the sign up under his chin, Lenny picked his way carefully down the stone steps; it was really hard to see through Rozzie's dark glasses.

Which is probably why he never knew how Mousie Blatner suddenly happened to appear at the iron railing just as Lenny reached the bottom of the steps.

"Hey, what're you dressed up for? Halloween? Haw haw!"

Lenny heard himself give a strangled little cry as he tripped off the last step and stumbled right into Mousie Blatner's hulking frame.

"Have a nice trip? Haw haw!"

Lenny clutched at his sign and listened to the sounds his heart made as it hammered in his chest. He wondered, briefly, if he was about to have a heart attack, and if so, would it be less painful to die that way than with Mousie's hamlike hands closing around his throat?

"Gonna have a show, huh? What're you, the dog act? Haw haw."

Suddenly, incredibly, it dawned on Lenny that Mousie Blatner did not recognize him. He didn't sound mad or threatening or dangerous or anything like he should have sounded if he'd known who Lenny was.

Either the disguise was working or in the darkened movie theater Mousie had never really gotten a good look at him!

111

Little squeaking sounds came from Lenny's mouth as he tried to talk. He knew he should say something, but he was afraid that Mousie might recognize his voice.

"Maybe you're the cat act," Mousie guffawed. "You sound like a little kitty cat."

Lenny took a breath. "Ho ho," he said, trying to make his voice deep and rich. "That's a good one on me."

"When's the show?" Mousie asked. "Maybe I'll come."

"Oh, it's not going to be much of a show." The last thing he needed was Mousie Blatner in the audience. Mousie might recognize him without the mustache and sunglasses.

"When is it?" Mousie repeated.

Lenny grasped at a straw of hope. If Mousie was too stupid to notice that he was carrying a sign advertising the show, maybe he was also too stupid to know how to read.

"It's on the sign," he said.

"You're holding the sign upside down," Mousie said. "Boy, are you dumb. How's anybody gonna be able to read your sign if you're holding it upside down?"

"I guess I better stand on my head," Lenny said. "Ho ho ho."

Mousie reached out, grabbed the sign from Lenny's hands, and turned it right side up. "Two o'clock Sunday. What Sunday?"

"N–next Sunday," Lenny said, forgetting to deepen his voice. What quick thinking! His father would have been proud of him. "You need brains as well as brawn," he'd say. "It's good to be brave, but it's better to be smart *and* brave."

Lenny didn't remember his father ever actually saying that, but he was sure it sounded like something he would have said, if he'd had a chance.

"Next Sunday," he repeated. "Don't forget. Not this Sunday."

He took the sign back, held his breath as he turned away from Mousie, and walked toward the center of the schoolyard. When he didn't feel Mousie's big hand clamp down on his shoulder, Lenny let his breath out with a whoosh.

That was a close call.

Mousie hadn't recognized him in his disguise, and for all he knew, Mousie would never recognize him—but whichever it was, at least Lenny was no longer facing imminent death. He would carry his sign and wear his disguise to and from school every day, as an advertising gimmick for the show this Sunday.

And if Mousie did decide to come to the show, when Lenny wouldn't be wearing his disguise, he'd come *next* Sunday.

And who'd be up on the roof next Sunday?

Nobody.
Especially not Lenny.

By Saturday, so many kids were talking about Lenny's show that Lenny was beginning to picture *two* cigar boxes overflowing with dimes.

Lenny had managed to sneak Rozzie's sunglasses back without being caught and decided he'd better not press his luck. So for the rest of the week he wore a big rubber nose and fake glasses that Artie had used on Halloween. With these, plus a baseball cap turned backwards on his head, he'd attracted a lot of attention.

Saturday morning Lenny and Artie tacked up crayon-printed signs on trees and lampposts all over the neighborhood. There was no telling how many people would come.

"Fifty people is five dollars." Lenny said excitedly. "And if a hundred people come, that's ten dollars—and if I do this every week—at ten dollars a week—holy moley, Artie, my troubles are over!"

"It might be hard to come up with a new act every week," Artie said.

"Aw, you know me, Artie. I got a million of 'em." Lenny paused as he remembered Mousie Blatner. "Maybe we better skip next Sunday, though."

Lenny had been rehearsing his act all week and could hardly wait for tomorrow. It wasn't only the money—in fact, though he liked to close his eyes and see all those dimes spilling out of the cigar boxes, he was even more excited at the thought of beginning his career at last.

Who knew what might happen after tomorrow? Word might get around that there was a talented young comedian—very young comedian—performing for dimes on a rooftop in Flushing. Maybe a famous agent or talent scout who had nothing to do one Sunday afternoon would decide to take in Lenny's show— just for laughs.

Or maybe the newspapers would hear about him and send a reporter to do a—what was it they called it?—a "human interest story" on Lenny. And somebody big and important in show business would read the story and—

Why, there was no telling what this could lead to!

And even if nobody famous in show business came to see him perform, if a hundred kids came every week, he'd be practically rolling in dimes! But whatever happened, at least Lenny was finally on the road to his dream, with his first public appearance only a day away, and stardom almost within sight at the end of the road.

Saturday felt like it would drag on forever.

116

Artie asked Lenny if he wanted to go to the movies, but Lenny thought it might be a better idea to avoid the movies today, just in case Mousie Blatner was there.

Artie was torn between keeping Lenny company or missing Chapter Four of *Lost City of the Jungle*.

"Listen, you go if you want," Lenny said. "There's a Dodger game on anyway. You don't have to stay home just because I do."

"It's no fun going alone," Artie said.

"But if neither of us goes, we won't know what happens in *Lost City of the Jungle*," Lenny pointed out.

"Yeah, that's true."

Artie finally decided to go, and Lenny had just enough time to rehearse his act once more before the ballgame started.

There was no one else home. Lenny's mother was working at Annette's and Rozzie was out shopping. Lenny went into the bathroom and turned on the light. He stood on tiptoe in front of the mirror.

"And now, ladies and gentlemen, the person you've been waiting all week for, the one, the only—LENNY DELL!"

"Thank you, thank you, you're a wonderful audience. I just wanna tell you—"

The front door opened. "Lenny? Lenny, come here!"

Rozzie was home. So much for rehearsing.

Now he'd have to help her put away the groceries.

He sighed and went into the foyer. Rozzie was standing there with the metal shopping cart right inside the door, holding a piece of paper in her hand.

"What is this?" she demanded. "What do you think you're doing?"

"I think I'm standing here in the foyer," Lenny said. "What do *you* think I'm doing?"

"Don't be a smart aleck, Lenny. What is this?" She held out the paper.

"Say, you're over there, I'm over here. How do I know what you've got over there?"

But suddenly Lenny realized he did know.

"Oh, that."

"Oh, that," Rozzie mimicked. "Yes, that. What was this doing on the lamppost on the corner?"

"Hey, why'd you take it down? That's our advertising."

"Advertising for what?"

"Can't you read? For my show, that's what."

"You can't put on a show on the roof, for heaven's sake. It's not your roof, you know."

"Why can't I? Is there a law against it? It's as much my roof as anybody else's."

"But it's everybody's roof," Rozzie said. "Everybody in the building. They won't like it."

118

"Why not? How do you know they won't come to the show and have a lot of fun?"

"What kind of a show could you put on?" Rozzie sneered.

"I'm going to tell jokes," Lenny said. "And I'm very funny. Everybody says so. All the kids in school are coming. They know how funny I am."

"I'll bet," Rozzie muttered.

"You and Ma are the only ones who don't think I can be a famous comedian. Why don't you come and see for yourself?"

"Well, I still don't think they'll let you do it," Rozzie said. "And I don't think you should put signs up all over the place with our address on them. What'll my friends think?"

"They'll think, hey, Rozzie's brother is famous."

"I know Ma isn't going to like this," Rozzie said. "You wait. She's not going to like it one bit."

"Then *you* come to my show," Lenny said. "It'll cost you a dime," he added.

Rozzie was right.

Lenny's mother didn't like the idea at all. She was carrying one of Lenny's signs when she came home from work, and the first thing she did, even before she took off her sweater, was to wave it under his face and demand, "What's the meaning of this?"

Lenny explained. He thought she would understand better or at least make less of a fuss about it, if he talked about the cigar box full of dimes.

"Because I have to pay to get Aunt Harriet's fur cleaned"—and maybe fixed, he added silently—"and Rozzie said I was too young to baby-sit, and I can't earn enough money selling papers or collecting soda bottles and I don't know anybody who's made money selling Cloverine Salve and they probably don't have encyclopedia salesboys. And because I'm a good comedian and everybody knows it but you, so I knew a lot of kids would pay to hear me tell jokes."

"You don't tell them jokes for nothing all the time?" his mother said.

"Sure I do. That's how come they know I'm such a good comedian and that's how come they all want to see the show."

"Lenny, Lenny, this crazy idea you have that you'll be a comedian—why can't you be realistic? That's no kind of a life, show business. There's no security, no stability—ninety-nine percent of the people who think they're going to be big stars end up starving."

"I know, Ma," Lenny sighed. "You tell me that all the time."

"You don't listen any of the time!"

"Because it's what I like best, and it's what I'm good at. You were always complaining that

Pop sold shoes, and he was too good to sell shoes. I'll bet he wasn't happy doing that. Not when he was so smart. That's what you always said."

Her eyes flashed dangerously. "How do you know what I said to your father? You're too young to even remember."

"Oh no I'm not!" Lenny said. "I remember."

"Well, you're too smart to be a joke teller. You have a perfectly good brain—"

"Oh, I don't know about that," Rozzie said.

"Butt out, Rosalind!" her mother snapped. "Lenny, you could make something of yourself if you used that brain once in a while. But no, you spend your time thinking up wisecracks, daydreaming about how you're going to be a famous star. Meanwhile, you're getting N's on your report card, sneaking around with your Aunt Harriet's fur scarf, getting dragged home by the police—"

"Are you gonna dig up my whole past?" Lenny cried. "All we're talking about is one show I'm doing tomorrow!"

"And making a spectacle of yourself like a street beggar for pennies!"

Lenny didn't know whether to scream or cry. He fumed with frustration because his mother was carrying on as if he wanted to do something awful, but at the same time there was a terrible sadness in knowing she didn't appreciate—in fact, despised—the very thing that Lenny cherished most.

He tried to stay calm and sound reasonable. "I'll be on the roof, not the street, and I won't be begging, I'll be doing a comedy act, and it's not for pennies, it's for dimes."

Mrs. Kandell started to say something, then stopped. She crumpled Lenny's paper sign in her fist and turned away.

"You must be tired, Ma," Rozzie said. "Come on, I'll make you some coffee. And don't worry so much. Maybe it's just a stage. Maybe he'll grow out of it."

Lenny wanted to shout, "I'LL NEVER GROW OUT OF IT!" but he knew better than to start up again. He was grateful to his sister who was sort of pushing his mother along into the kitchen now, and he guessed it really didn't matter what Rozzie said, as long as it calmed her down.

Mrs. Kandell stopped in the doorway of the kitchen and turned around.

"Who said you had to pay for cleaning Aunt Harriet's fur?"

For a moment Lenny was so startled he didn't say anything.

Then he blurted out, "You did!"

"I never said any such thing. I said I'd pay for it. How could you pay for it? You don't have any money."

"But—but—"

"And they won't take any money from me, because Joe said it gets cleaned when Harriet puts it in storage for the summer. So it's not costing them anything. Not that they couldn't afford it. I don't even know why she hangs on to that ratty scarf. For what it costs to repair it, she could put the money toward a mink."

"Repair it?" Lenny squeaked.

"It's so old the skins are coming apart—or the pelts—whatever you call those things. Every year they separate, and every year she has it repaired. I personally think it was a piece of junk in the first place, and I don't know why she—Lenny sagged against a dinette chair. Was the room actually whirling around, or was he just light-headed with relief? He'd never stabbed the fur at all! There'd been a hole in it before he ever sneaked it out of the house!

"Ma," he began weakly. "Ma, why didn't you tell me—" All this time he'd thought he'd have to pay heaven-only-knew-what for cleaning and/or fixing the scarf, and all this time— "Why didn't you tell me you didn't have to pay to get the scarf cleaned? Why didn't you tell me it wasn't going to cost us anything?"

"What am I, a mind reader?" his mother said. "You never asked me. I thought you forgot all about it. Since when are you such a worrier, anyway?"

"Coffee's ready," Rozzie said.

Lenny couldn't believe it. Two weeks of

worrying, wondering, and waiting, and all for nothing!

Well, maybe not for nothing. He wasn't thinking too clearly, and he still felt a sort of dazed disbelief, but Lenny realized that if he hadn't spent a good part of the last two weeks trying to figure out how he was going to pay for Aunt Harriet's stoned marten, he probably would never have come up with the idea for his show.

"Holy moley," he breathed. "I'm gonna get to keep all that money!"

Think of the dress he could buy Georgina! And there'd probably be plenty left over, too.

If Mousie Blatner didn't recognize him all his troubles were over! And if he did, Lenny would probably have enough money to skip town. Maybe he wouldn't be able to get as far as Australia, but he was pretty sure he'd be able to afford a bus to Atlantic City.

TEN

LENNY STOOD AT THE IRON DOOR as his audience gathered on his rooftop theater.

If only I had a white tux, Lenny thought, everything would be perfect.

Well, maybe not exactly perfect.

There were no chairs on the roof, so the audience had to sit right on the hot tar surface, and some of the girls squealed when they squatted, and a couple complained that they were going to get their dresses dirty.

And Lenny had to collect the money himself, because Artie was standing downstairs inside the lobby, letting the kids in so they wouldn't be punching people's apartment buzzers to get the lobby door open.

And Lenny would have to do his own introduction, because Artie said he would be too nervous to talk in front of a big audience like that.

But the sun was shining like a spotlight, and none of the kids were trying to get by him without paying, and none of the girls were leaving, and it was going to be a big audience.

The Elmhurst Dairy crate was still there. Lenny told everyone that it was the stage, and the audience was forming into sort of a horse-shoe around it, giggling and chattering and looking over toward Lenny, yelling, "When's the show gonna start?"

Lenny didn't have a watch, but Artie did, and they'd planned that Artie would come up at two o'clock and give Lenny the high sign to start. Unless there were a whole lot of kids still coming; then Artie said he'd wait a few minutes more, just to make sure everyone could get in.

"Pretty soon now," Lenny said. It must be close to two o'clock, he thought. The cigar box wasn't exactly overflowing with dimes, but there were about thirty kids in the audience already. No one who came through the iron roof-door looked at all like a show-business big shot—in fact, there were no adults at all, but it was unreasonable to expect a talent scout to be there the first time. Word hadn't gotten around yet.

It was just as well. This would be the first time he tested his act on a real, live audience.

A talent scout showing up now would just put too much pressure on him.

Not that Lenny had stage fright. (Or dairy-crate fright, he thought, chuckling). He felt pretty good. Excited, eager to get started . . . maybe just a little bit nervous. But it was a good kind of nervousness. It made him feel tingly and alert and full of energy.

"Thank you, thank you, the stage is over there, the show's about to start in just a few minutes, pull up a piece of roof and sit down."

"Thank you, thank you." Lenny kept up a steady stream of patter as bunches of kids came through the door and dropped their dimes into the cigar box.

Lenny looked toward the stage. There must be forty people on the roof!

He turned as he heard two more dimes hit the cigar box. "Thank you, th—"

Lenny gaped. Georgina Schultz stood in the doorway, holding on to a little kid with a huge red sucker. She tilted her head and gave Lenny a haughty stare. "My little brother wanted to come." She marched off toward the semicircle of kids around the dairy crate.

Lenny gazed after her, hardly believing she was there. Even though she'd looked interested from the first moment the show was mentioned, Lenny hadn't really expected her to come. He thought she was too mad at him, and too proud to give him the satisfaction.

Lenny wasn't falling for that "my little brother" line. The kid was hardly old enough to walk, let alone read a sign on a lamppost.

Wait till she sees the dress I'm going to get her! Lenny thought. Wait till she finds out that practically all this is for her!

"Hey, when's the show gonna start? We want the show! We want the show!"

The kids began clapping and chanting. Lenny waved an arm at them. "Just a couple minutes more, folks. It's not two o'clock yet."

"It is too! It's ten after. WE WANT THE SHOW ! WE WANT THE SHOW!"

"Okay, okay, keep your shirts on. We're just about ready to—"

"WE WANT THE SHOW *NOW!* WE WANT THE SHOW *NOW!"*

"All right already!" Lenny put the cigar box down next to the iron door. He wondered, briefly, why Artie hadn't come up to the roof yet.

But Lenny had kept his audience waiting long enough. There was no time to wonder where Artie was, no time to wonder whether he would have stage fright.

It was show time. Lenny took a deep breath.

"And now, ladies and gentlemen, the moment you've all been waiting for. Here he is, that talented comedian, that star of stage, screen, and roof, the one, the only—ME!" He sprinted over to the Elmhurst Dairy crate and swooped down in an exaggerated bow, to show the audience that the introduction was supposed to be sort of a joke, and not meant to be conceited.

The audience clapped politely. Lenny jumped onto the dairy crate and stood for a moment, just looking out at the expectant, upturned faces. He felt a surge of excitement, as if he was suddenly charged with electricity, and he knew it was because this was how it felt when a dream finally came true.

He thought he could almost spring off the dairy crate and go flying around the roof like Superman. And when he started to talk, all the confidence and vitality that he felt pulsing through his veins charged his voice with a power that projected it booming across the roof.

"I want to thank me for that very kind introduction," he said. The kids tittered.

"And let me tell you, it's a miracle I'm here at all. What a week I had. My teacher asked me how come geese fly south in the winter. I said, 'Why not—it's too far to walk.' Then she asked me to use the words *defeat, deduct, defense,* and *detail* in one sentence. So I said, 'Defeat of deduct go over defense before detail.' "

The kids giggled appreciatively. Lenny was just warming up.

"To top it all off, she asks me, 'What's the difference between prose and poetry.' So I say,

'There was a young man named Glass,/Who went wading up to his knees.' And she asks, 'Is that prose or poetry?' And I say, 'That's prose—but if the water was a little higher, it would be poetry.' "

Some of the kids didn't get it, but the ones who did hooted with laughter.

"What a week," Lenny went on. "Last night my mother wakes me up at two in the morning, screaming that there's a mouse in her bedroom. I go into her room to look, and I say, 'I don't see any mouse.' And she says, 'I'm telling you, there was a mouse in here, I heard it squeaking.' So I said, 'Well, what do you want me to do, oil it?' "

There was an encouraging burst of giggles. Lenny knew enough not to start out with your best stuff, but to build up to it, holding out the really boffo jokes for the big finish.

"Then yesterday I went for a drive in the country with my Uncle Fred. Well, the car broke down and he went out to look under the hood, and this old horse comes trotting by. And the horse says, 'Neighhh. Better check the gas line.' And he trots off.

"Well, my uncle is the nervous type, and he gets so frightened, we run to the nearest farmhouse. He tells the farmer what happened, and the farmer says, 'Was this an old horse with one floppy ear?' And my uncle says, 'Yeah,

yeah.' And the farmer says, 'Aw, don't pay any attention to him. He doesn't know a thing about cars.'

"And speaking of horses, did you hear the one about the horse who walked into a restaurant and ordered a steak two inches thick with sour cream and caraway seeds on top of it, and sliced onions on top of that, and then on top of the onions a piece of tomato and an artichoke with a cherry in the middle? Well, the waiter goes to the kitchen and brings the horse the steak and the horse eats it and says to the waiter, 'Say, didn't you think it was strange for me, a horse, to come in here and order a steak two inches thick with sour cream and caraway seeds and sliced onions and tomato and an artichoke with a cherry in the middle?"

"And the waiter says, 'What's so strange about that? I like my steak the same way.' "

More laughter. The audience was really warmed up now, and so was Lenny. He picked out Georgina's face. She was grinning, but when she saw him looking at her, she bit her lip and began fussing over her little brother.

Lenny smiled broadly. She wasn't fooling him a bit!

"Thank you, thank you. But let me tell you some more about my Uncle Fred. Like I said, my Uncle Fred is a really nervous type, and he was driving his wife to the hospital to have a baby and he was so nervous about getting her there in time that he lost control of the car and drove into a tree."

The roof door opened and Lenny saw Artie come in. Lenny grinned at him and Artie closed the door quietly behind him and tiptoed toward the audience. Artie looked sort of— nervous, or sick or something. Lenny only had time to wonder briefly what was wrong, and to hope Artie was okay. The kids were leaning forward, waiting for him to go on.

"So the next thing he knows, my uncle is in a hospital bed, and wakes up yelling, 'My wife! My wife! Is my wife okay?' And the doctor comes rushing in and says, 'Your wife's fine, and congratulations, you're the proud father of twins. A girl and a boy. They're fine too. The only thing is, you were unconscious for ten days after the accident, and your wife was unconscious for two days, and we had to get names for the birth certificates, so your wife's brother named the babies.'

"And my uncle says, 'Oh, no, my wife's brother is an idiot! I can just imagine the names he picked out.' And the doctor says, 'He named the girl Denise.' And my uncle says, 'Hey, Denise? That's not bad. That's kind of pretty. Denise. Okay, what did he name the boy?'

"And the doctor said, 'DeNephew.' "

Even Georgina laughed out loud now, and

she didn't try to hide it. Lenny felt the warmth of the sun and the warmth of his audience's response, and wished, just for a minute, that Rozzie and his mother were there to see him; to see for themselves that his dream wasn't crazy, that it really could come true.

Lenny told joke after joke, not waiting for the laughter to completely die down between punch lines, but just starting another story while the kids were still giggling. And the laughter built and built, getting harder and louder, the way he'd planned it, till Lenny was so flushed with success and self-confidence that he stopped wondering why Artie kept glancing nervously at the roof door.

Georgina had her little brother on her lap now, and was resting her chin on his head and gazing attentively at Lenny. Her mouth was slightly open and her golden curls were gently bobbing against her brother's temples.

Briefly Lenny wondered how Georgina's hair would feel brushing against his cheek.

Oh murder, Lenny thought, none of that now! He closed his eyes for a moment to shake off the sudden, vivid image of Georgina's cheek so close to his.

He heard a metallic *thunk* and opened his eyes. The roof door swung out, and there, at the top of the stairwell, frozen for one eternal moment like an ancient statue of vengeance, stood Mousie Blatner.

133

ELEVEN

LATER LENNY WOULD REMEMBER it all through a kind of hazy curtain of unreality. Even when people talked about it, it would seem like one of those misty dreams where you go through the motions and action of the dream but, at the same time, are somehow standing off to one side, watching everything that's happening to you.

"You're Lenny Kandell!" Mousie yelled. "You was Lenny Kandell all along."

All Lenny could see were the backs of heads, as his audience watched Mousie advance toward the stage. A few braver kids dared a "Shush! You're ruining the show," but mostly they just watched in fascination, as if Mousie were part of the act.

"I owe you somethin, Lenny Kandell, and now you're gonna get it."

Suddenly Lenny was aware of a strange, almost unnatural calm settling over him; as if he had already faced the worst terror imaginable and had somehow gotten beyond it and reached a distant point where he didn't recognize the familiar sensations of fear.

In fact, he felt hardly any sensation at all, except a distinct irritation at Mousie for interrupting his act.

"You owe me a dime if you want to see this show," Lenny said.

Out of the corner of his eye, Lenny saw Artie cringe. He thought, absently, that Artie was looking a little green.

"A smart aleck, aren't you?" Mousie sneered.

"It's better than being a dumb *Maurice*." There were barely repressed giggles from the audience, even when Mousie glared around at the kids and sputtered, "You shut up if you know what's good for you!"

"Thank you, thank you," Lenny said. He bowed. "You're a wonderful audience." Mousie was wading through the semicircle of kids now, moving heavily, menacingly toward the Elmhurst Dairy crate.

Lenny watched Mousie come toward him with his huge fists clenched, and he had that strange, dreamlike feeling that he was watching himself watch Mousie come toward him. Here I am, he thought admiringly, and there's

Mousie, who's going to kill me in about one minute, and I'm still on stage making wisecracks and laughing in the face of death.

What a trooper I am! Lenny marveled. If only my father could see me now.

And then, Mouse was two feet away from Lenny's stage, and Lenny saw him lower his shoulder in preparation for a flying tackle, and Lenny jumped off the dairy crate and ran to the edge of the roof.

"Hah! Ya coward!" Mousie yelled. "Ya sniveling yellow coward! Come on and fight like a man."

Lenny never did remember how he actually did it, or even why, but the next thing he knew, he was standing on the ledge of the roof, six stories above the ground, arms folded across his chest, and snarling, "You wanna fight? Come and get me, Blatner."

He had a moment to consider adding a Jimmy Cagney impression to his act before the shrieking started.

All the kids were on their feet now—some screaming for him to get down, some just mutely staring.

Mousie squinted up at him, shading his eyes from the sun with his hand. He didn't seem to know what to do next.

"What're you, crazy? Get down from there and fight."

"Come on up here and fight," Lenny yelled. "I dare you. Come on, if you're so brave, *Maurice*. Let's see you do this." And Lenny started slowly, carefully, to walk the ledge.

Don't look down, he told himself. Don't look down. He remembered the times he'd merely stood at the edge of the roof, remembered the scary sensation he'd felt looking down six stories to the sidewalk.

And now, here I am, he thought hazily, doing probably the scariest thing anybody can do, liable to fall off and plunge to my death if a little breeze comes up or I lose my footing. Boy, this audience is certainly getting their money's worth!

I better be really careful, Lenny thought. He swayed a little, but regained his balance. He wondered if one of the screams he heard was Georgina's.

"You're crazy!" Mousie howled.

"Yeah, that's right, Mousie, he is," Artie cried. "He's deranged. You better get out of here. He's got dementia praecox and you never know what he's going to do next."

"I'm not crazy!" Lenny called blithely. Oh yes I am, he thought. I'm walking around the edge of a roof, six stories off the ground. Seven, if you count the roof as an extra floor. Keep walking, he told himself, and don't look down. Remember how it feels when you look

down. No, don't remember! Don't even think about that. Just keep going. Anyway, it's not like being on a tightrope. The ledge is plenty wide enough. It's at least eighteen inches.

"That's the sure sign of an insane person!" Artie yelled. "When they say they're not crazy. Lenny!" Artie's voice cracked. "Get off there! You'll kill yourself!"

"I'm waiting, *Maurice,*" Lenny sang out cheerily. Slowly, carefully, he continued his walk. "Come and get me." Boy, he thought, my father ought to see this. I bet this would make him proud of me.

Then, in a dazzling flash of insight that he would remember even when he couldn't remember anything else about that afternoon, Lenny thought: This isn't brave, this is *stupid!* What am I *doing* up here? He stopped walking and stood on the ledge, paralyzed with indecision.

What in the world do I do now?

At that moment, a whole lot of things happened at once.

Mousie Blatner howled, "I'm gettin' outta here, you're outta your effin' mind!"

A familiar scream pierced the air. "LENNY! WHAT ARE YOU DOING UP THERE?" He'd know Rozzie's scream anywhere.

And Uncle Joe's voice, sounding unfamiliar because of an odd quaver in it, as if he were talking under water. "Don't startle him, don't make any sudden movements. Lenny, Lenny, don't do it!"

And his entire body breaking out in a cold, prickly, sickening sweat, as all the sensations of terror and reality returned in a dizzying whoosh, and he swayed and pitched forward and the black tar surface of the roof came rushing up to meet him.

"Why? *Why?*"

"I don't know why. But I'll bet old Mousie Blatner won't bother me again."

"He's crazy," his mother wailed. "Joe, he's crazy. He's raving."

Lenny sat on the couch, sipping at a glass of Manischewitz Concord Grape wine. Artie sat on a chair across from him, leaning forward, watching him swallow. Artie's gaze was unblinking, as if Lenny might vanish into thin air if Artie took his eyes off him for a moment.

The wine was nice and sweet and wasn't doing a thing to clear Lenny's head. He wasn't sure why they were giving it to him, except that Uncle Joe had told his mother to give him some brandy, and Mrs. Kandell said they didn't have any brandy, they only had Manischewitz.

"He's not really crazy," Artie said, turning

toward Mrs. Kandell for a moment. "I just said he had dementia praecox to scare Mousie."

"Good work," Lenny said.

"You're not, are you?" Artie whispered nervously.

"Not what?" Lenny took another sip of wine.

"Crazy?"

"I think he's crazy," Rozzie shrilled. "You have to be crazy to walk on the ledge of a roof."

"This is what happened," Lenny said, as if making an important announcement. "This kid was coming to kill me. I was doing my show, which none of you bothered to come to, and which was very good, wasn't it, Artie?"

"Nobody asked for their money back," Artie said.

"There, you see? Anyhow, this kid came to kill me and I got up and walked on the ledge and told him to come and get me."

"Why?" Everybody shouted it at once.

"I'm not sure," Lenny admitted. "It seemed like a good idea at the time. I was thinking about my father . . ." Lenny's voice got faraway and dreamy. ". . . about how brave he was, and how he'd want me to be brave . . . and if he could face Japs and Germans and not be afraid, he'd want me to face Mousie Blatner and not be afraid . . ."

Aunt Harriet looked as though she was about to explode. She twisted a handkerchief in her fingers and her face got redder and redder.

". . . only Mousie really would have killed me if I tried to fight him, so I—"

"Your father never fought anybody!" Aunt Harriet shrieked. "Your father was killed falling down a gangway on a troop ship! He never even got overseas!"

"For God's sake, Harriet!" Uncle Joe roared.

Lenny sat calmly sipping wine as the voices erupted around him. Artie's mouth had dropped open; he looked in stunned confusion at Lenny, then at Aunt Harriet.

". . . told him a million times, but he insists—"

"Harriet, it's none of your business!" Mrs. Kandell's voice cut through the babble. "You have no right—"

"You're the one who always says how senseless it was—"

"He was *my* husband, Harriet! It was *my* loss. And Lenny is *my* son. If he thinks of his father as a hero, are you going to say he's wrong?"

Rozzie huddled in a corner and started to cry. Uncle Joe paced back and forth around Aunt Harriet's chair, hitting one of his palms

142

with the clenched fist of his other hand. Lenny wondered if his uncle wanted to punch Aunt Harriet. He hoped he would.

"You're the one who always said he was wrong, Ida. And his father too—"

"Harriet!" Uncle Joe's voice was threatening. "Harriet, *shut up!*"

"And you know something else, Harriet?" Lenny's mother went on. "If Lenny remembers his father with love and admiration, and looks up to him like a hero, is that such a terrible thing? Who does it hurt? How is it better for him to know the exact details of—"

Maybe it was the wine making him dizzy, or the clamoring voices giving him the headache, or leftover shock from realizing he could have killed himself an hour ago, but suddenly Lenny found himself ready to say something he had never said before, never out loud, never to anyone, and certainly never in front of Artie.

"I know."

They all turned to look at him. Their silence was a relief. Lenny was really feeling tired.

He'd known all along. It had never been a secret that his father had died on the troop ship. Did they really think he didn't know? With all the talking and arguing that had gone on among them for the past four years, Lenny would have had to be an idiot—or *really* crazy—not to know the truth.

"Lenny." Uncle Joe bent down and put his hand on his shoulder. "Lenny, if you knew, why—"

"You think he wanted to die that way?" Lenny said, very loudly. "He sold shoes. He *sold shoes*. Then he went to fight Hitler. If he had to die, he'd rather have died being a hero. So that's the way I tell it."

Lenny hauled himself off the couch. He handed the wineglass to Artie.

"You can finish it," he said. "I don't want any more."

TWELVE

LENNY HAD MADE $4.20 FROM HIS show. If he gave one more performance, he'd have enough to buy Georgina a really expensive dress.

The whole school was buzzing with the details of his daring roof walk when he and Artie got there Monday morning.

"Boy, talk about publicity!" said Lenny. "I'll bet we get a hundred kids for the next show!"

"Yeah, but they might be disconsolate if you don't walk on the ledge again," Artie said.

"I might be disconsolate if I do," Lenny said. "Uh—mightn't I?"

"You might be *dead*."

"Hey, look, there's Mousie Blatner. Way over there. Look, Artie, he sees me. Say, he's turning the other way, look at that! I think he's avoiding me! Hey, Artie, let's go over and—"

"Lenny, don't press your luck."

"Okay, okay."

Artie was a good kid, Lenny thought, and very understanding. He hadn't asked Lenny anything about what he'd said yesterday, about his father, or why Lenny had told him his father was a war hero.

Someday I'll explain it to him, Lenny thought. One day when I want to talk about it some more.

They marched upstairs and into the classroom. Lenny paused at Miss Randolph's desk.

"Hey, Miss Randolph? How many successful jumps does a paratrooper have to make before he's allowed to go into combat?"

Miss Randolph raised her head. Lenny thought she looked a little startled. *I got her, I got her!* He leaned forward eagerly, ready to spring the answer on her.

Miss Randolph frowned, gazed off toward the window. Lenny was just about to yell, "Give up? Give up?" when Miss Randolph's eyes brightened and she smiled triumphantly.

"All of them. Take your seat please, Leonard."

"Darn!" he groaned. "Darn, darn, *darn!*"

He sat down at his desk. Georgina, whose seat was three rows away, was walking toward him. She looked back at Miss Randolph, who was writing on the blackboard, then leaned down to whisper in Lenny's ear.

"You're crazy, Lenny Kandell, you know that? I never saw anyone do such a crazy thing in my life as you did yesterday. You could have gotten *killed.*"

"That's show biz," Lenny cracked.

"Well, don't you do it again," she whispered sternly.

Lenny gulped.

As Georgina straightened up, one of her long, golden curls brushed clear across Lenny's cheek.

Oh murder . . .

About the Author

Ellen Conford is the author of many popular books that have established her as an award-winning writer for young readers. Her book *And This is Laura* has been made into an ABC-TV *Weekend Special* as "The Girl With ESP." Another book, *Hail, Hail Camp Timberwood* won the Pacific Northwest Library Association Young Readers' Choice Award and the California Young Reader Medal in the junior high category.

Lenny Kandell, Smart Aleck was selected as a *School Library Journal* Best Book and has won a *Parent's Choice* Award for Literature.

Ms. Conford writes three to five hours a day—or ten pages, whichever comes first! Besides writing and reading, she also enjoys Scrabble, crossword puzzles, and old movies.

She went to school at Hofstra University and still enjoys taking classes when she has the time. She lives in Great Neck, New York with her husband—who is a college professor—a college-aged son, and a very lovable sheepdog.

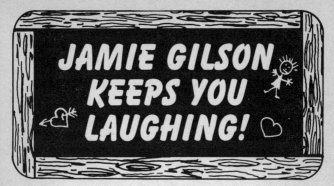

JAMIE GILSON KEEPS YOU LAUGHING!

Her books are filled with funny adventures, zany schemes and crazy situations that you could get yourself in to— and have to get out of!!

_____ **DON'T CATCH ME, I'M THE GINGERBREAD MAN** 44835/$1.95
Mitch is a hotshot hockey player, a health food nut, and a heavy favorite to win the Bake-a-Thon prize of $30,000!

_____ **DIAL LEROI RUPERT, DJ** 56099/$1.75
Three friends team up as a jazz combo and join their favorite deejay in a night of instant fame!

_____ **DO BANANAS CHEW GUM?** 42690/$1.95
It's not a riddle, it's a test. And since Sam can't read, it's not as easy as it looks!

_____ **THIRTEEN WAYS TO SINK A SUB** 47285/$1.95
Substitute teachers are fair game—and the boys and girls of Room 4B can't wait to play!

POCKET BOOKS, DEPT. GIL
1230 Avenue of the Americas, New York, N.Y. 10020

Please send me the books I have checked above. I am enclosing $_____ (please add 75¢ to cover postage and handling for each order. N.Y.S. and N.Y.C. residents please add appropriate sales tax.) Send check or money order—no cash or C.O.D.s please. Allow up to six weeks for delivery. For purchases over $10.00, you may use VISA: card number, expiration date and customer signature must be included.

NAME _____

ADDRESS _____

CITY _____ STATE/ZIP _____

☐ **Check here to receive your free Pocket Books order form.**   373